His mind was occupied with fantasies...

...of sliding her shirt off, feasting his eyes on her. Kellan couldn't answer, until she asked again. "Why did you look through your stepmother's things?"

"My father sent her a letter. I need to know what's in it. To understand why he left her his entire estate."

Irina glared at him. "It's none of your business, Kellan. I won't help you and I won't let you spy on her."

Irina stood between him and his mission, but it was good to see her again. Too good. He should have been past this. He'd stayed away from her for seven years. But distance hadn't been enough to erase her memory. She'd been in his dreams. In his every waking moment. Now she stood before him, real and enticing.

All he had to do was stay clear of her.

So why couldn't he walk away?

* * *

Tempting the Texan by *USA TODAY* bestselling author Maureen Child is part of the Texas Cattleman's Club: Inheritance series.

Dear Reader,

We're back to the Texas Cattlemen's Club. I do love coming back to these stories. Not only is it fun to connect with other writers and compare notes on the books as we go, but I love Royal, Texas, so writing a new story set there is a little like coming home for me.

In *Tempting the Texan,* you'll meet Kellan and Irina. They had quite the connection seven years ago, but then Kellan left town, chased by memories he couldn't get past.

Irina has built a good life while Kellan was gone, but she's never really forgotten him, either. Now that he's back, her lovely ordered world is spinning out of control.

And she likes it.

I really hope you enjoy this revisit to Royal! Please visit me on Facebook and let me know what you think!

Until the next time, happy reading!

Maureen Child

MAUREEN CHILD

—

TEMPTING THE TEXAN

PAPL
DISCARDED

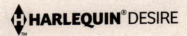

Special thanks and acknowledgment are given
to Maureen Child for her contribution to the
Texas Cattleman's Club: Inheritance miniseries.

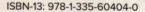

ISBN-13: 978-1-335-60404-0

Recycling programs
for this product may
not exist in your area.

Tempting the Texan

Printed in U.S.A.

www.Harlequin.com

Maureen Child writes for the Harlequin Desire line and can't imagine a better job. A seven-time finalist for the prestigious Romance Writers of America RITA® Award, Maureen is the author of more than one hundred romance novels. Her books regularly appear on bestseller lists and have won several awards, including a Prism Award, a National Readers' Choice Award, a Colorado Romance Writers Award of Excellence and a Golden Quill Award. She is a native Californian but has recently moved to the mountains of Utah.

Books by Maureen Child

Harlequin Desire

The Tycoon's Secret Child
A Texas-Sized Secret
Little Secrets: His Unexpected Heir
Rich Rancher's Redemption
Billionaire's Bargain
Tempt Me in Vegas
Bombshell for the Boss
Red Hot Rancher

Texas Cattleman's Club: Inheritance

Tempting the Texan

Visit her Author Profile page at Harlequin.com, or maureenchild.com, for more titles.

You can also find Maureen Child on Facebook, along with other Harlequin Desire authors, at Facebook.com/harlequindesireauthors!

To Harlequin Desire readers.
Thanks to you,
I can tell all the stories I love to read.
I appreciate you all so much.

Prologue

Kellan Blackwood was pissed.

His father, Buckley Blackwood, was dead and gone and yet the old man was still pulling strings. Only Buck could manage that from the grave.

Kel glanced at his brother and sister and silently admitted they didn't look any happier than he felt. Vaughn's intense green eyes were narrowed thoughtfully and he was half-sprawled in his chair. Sophie, their baby sister, wore black, and her long auburn hair was pulled back from her pretty face. Her brown eyes were teary, but she still looked as if she were torn between sorrow and anger.

Kel couldn't blame her. This wasn't easy on any of them, but there was no way to avoid what was coming. But at least they had each other to lean on. All three of them had had complicated "relationships" with their father. Buck had never been concerned with his kids or what they were doing. So the three of them, as children, had formed a tight bond that held strong today.

Kace LeBlanc, Buck's lawyer, walked into the office and stopped. "Kel," he said and nodded. "Vaughn. Sophie. Thanks for coming."

"Not like we had much choice, Kace." Vaughn sat up straight and tugged at the edges of his jacket.

"Right." Kace looked uncomfortable and Kel could understand it. As Buck's lawyer, Kace knew as well as they did that Buck hadn't given a good damn about his children—it was his businesses that had demanded his attention.

"Where's Miranda?" Kace glanced around the room as if expecting her to stand up from behind a chair.

"She hasn't managed to come downstairs yet," Kel explained, and his tone said exactly what he thought of the woman who had married and divorced his father.

Miranda Dupree was thirty-six years old. Same age as Kellan. A hell of a thing for your father to marry a woman the same age as his oldest child. But Buck had been a wealthy, lonely old man and she'd swooped in on his checkbook so fast, she'd been nothing but a redheaded blur. Sophie had given Miranda the nickname *Step-witch*, and Kel had to say it suited the grasping, greedy—

"Hello, everyone."

Speak of the devil, Kel thought. He stood because his mother had drilled manners into him from the time he was a child. Then he surreptitiously slapped Vaughn's shoulder to get him on his feet, as well. The one thing Kel couldn't manage was making his voice sound welcoming. "Miranda. Surprised to see you back in Royal."

The woman was beautiful, he'd give her that. Bright red hair, brilliant blue eyes and a figure that would bring some men—including his father—to their knees. But when Kel looked at her all he saw was the woman who'd driven another wedge between Buck and his family.

"Buck sent me a letter asking me to be here— along with a few other things." Miranda gave him a slow smile that he was willing to bet she practiced in front of a mirror. "From what I hear, you're not here all that often, either, Kellan. You live in Nashville now, don't you?"

He gritted his teeth to keep what he wanted to say to the woman locked inside. There were plenty of reasons for his move to Nashville several years ago. And not one of them was any of Miranda's business.

"Why are you even here?" Vaughn demanded. "Not like Buck's alive enough for you to seduce again."

"Like I said, Buck wanted me here," she said simply and took a seat, smoothing her tight black skirt over her thighs. Glancing over to Sophie and ignoring the men, she said, "I'm sorry about your father, Sophie."

"I am, too," she said and turned to look at Kace, in effect dismissing Miranda entirely.

"Can everyone just sit down?" Kace asked, his voice cool but clear.

"Yes," Sophie said, tugging on Vaughn's hand to get him back in his chair. "Come on, you guys, sit down and let's get this over with."

"Right," Kel agreed. No point in dragging this out. He wanted to settle his business and get out of Royal fast enough that he wouldn't run into—he cut that thought off because he couldn't afford to think about *her*. Not now. Not ever.

He scrubbed one hand across his whiskered jaw and told himself that raking up the past wouldn't serve anyone.

"Buck wanted all of you present to hear his will," Kace said from behind Buckley's desk. Instantly, Kel focused on the present.

"But it won't take long." Kace looked at each of them in turn, then zeroed in on Kellan. "I can give you all the legalese or just say it straight. Which do you want?"

Kel gave his siblings a quick look and nodded. They were clearly of a mind with him. He didn't give a damn what Miranda wanted. So he said, "Just say it, Kace."

Sympathy shone briefly in Kace's eyes and Kel knew he wasn't going to like whatever was coming before the man even said, "Basically, Buck left everything to Miranda."

"What?" Kellan was up and out of his chair in a blink. Vaughn was just a second or two behind him, and Sophie… Well, she sat there looking stunned as if she'd hit her head.

"You can't be serious." Kel glared at Kace.

"Yeah, I am." Kace didn't look happy about this. "He knew what he wanted and he laid it all out pretty clearly. And before you ask, your dad was of sound mind, Kellan," Kace said.

"You call this 'sound mind'?"

"Legally, yeah," Kace said. "I know this is hard—"

It was unthinkable. Buckley Blackwood hadn't been much of a father, but damned if Kellan could understand the old man leaving the family ranch to his ex-wife instead of his children. Slowly, he swiveled his head to stare at her. She didn't look surprised at all. Now, why was that? Had Kace told her what to expect? Had Buck?

"What the hell, Miranda?"

She shrugged and gave him that smile again. "I don't know why he did it, Kellan. All I know is he had a letter delivered to me after his death, telling me to be here for the will reading." She shrugged. "Your father was a generous man."

Not how Kellan remembered him.

"You know what? I didn't want his money or his property anyway," Vaughn said. "I don't need anything from him at this point. But there is no way

Dad would do this," Vaughn argued, glaring at their ex-stepmother.

"Yeah, well, he did," Kace said simply.

"He must have hated us," Sophie whispered.

"No," Kellan assured her. "He didn't." Hell, Buck hadn't noticed any of them enough to instill any real emotion—love or hate. Besides, no one could hate Sophie. "I don't know what the hell is going on," he said, giving Kace a hard glare before turning to Miranda. "But I will find out. For now, all I'll say is this isn't over."

One

Kel was still riding a tidal wave of righteous anger when he pulled up in front of the ranch house. Blackwood Hollow was a six-hundred-acre working ranch but the main building looked like a five-star luxury hotel. Sprawling twin wings spread out across the land and climbed to two stories. Lights shone in every window, making the whole place sparkle in the darkness. And with the white Christmas lights strung along the outline of the ranch house, it looked magical.

It was a mammoth place. His little sister, Sophie, sometimes stayed there, but they'd all gotten into the habit of avoiding Blackwood Hollow because they hadn't wanted to see Buck. A part of him wondered if that would change now that Buck was gone.

For Kellan, the memories in Royal were too hard, too painful to welcome him back for anything longer than a short visit to see his siblings even if that meant an extra trip into Dallas to see Vaughn.

Frowning, Kel looked past the main house to the guest quarters. Just as luxurious, the stone-and-glass building held four guest suites, a massive great room and a four-car garage.

"And," he murmured, "not a chance Miranda's staying there."

His father's ex wouldn't settle for anything less than the big house. Especially now, since she apparently *owned* it.

Okay, there was the rage again, in a fresh wave that nearly stole his breath. Shaking his head, he got out of his black Range Rover and headed for the main house. A couple of the ranch hands nodded or lifted a hand in greeting, but didn't try to stop him to chat. Good call.

He was here only because he knew the Step-witch wasn't. His sister, Sophie, had called him to say that Miranda was in town, shopping. Naturally. When you inherit several billion dollars, you want to spend some of it.

Muttering under his breath, Kellan entered the house, crossed the foyer and walked into the great room. He gave a quick look around, to assure himself she wasn't there. He hardly noticed the blazing fire in the hearth or the dark brown leather sofas and chairs clustered in conversational groups.

Deliberately, he kept his gaze off the damn Christmas tree in front of the bank of windows overlooking the front yard. It glittered and shone with multicolored lights and ribbons of silver and gold. The scent of pine hung in the air and stirred more memories, whether he wanted them or not. As a kid, he'd loved this house during the Christmas season because his mother had always gone all out on decorating.

The holidays were always opulent at Blackwood Hollow. It was the one tradition even Buck had kept after Kel's mother and he had divorced. Donna-Leigh had died a few years ago, but here at Blackwood Hollow Kel could still feel her influence. Tiny lights were strung around every window and there were decorated trees in almost every room of the house. The whole place smelled like evergreen, and as the memories rushed into his mind, Kel fought to keep them out.

He reminded himself that almost before the ink on their divorce decree had dried, Buck had married Miranda DuPree and brought her into the house that had been Donna-Leigh's. So the old man keeping Kel's mother's decorating traditions alive didn't mean squat.

Quickly, he took the stairs to the second story, ignoring the decorated tree on the landing and the twinkling white lights strung along the hallway. He checked the first of the guest rooms. Empty. No sign of anyone staying there. He moved on down the hall, his footsteps muffled on the dark red runner laid out in the center of the gleaming oak floor. Next room. Still nothing. He was down to two now. He didn't know how long Miranda would be in town, though according to Sophie, the woman was being trailed all through Royal by the camera crew that worked on the ridiculous TV show she was on.

Secret Lives of NYC Ex-Wives.

He snorted. So she'd found a way to make even more money out of her divorce from a rich man. And now her costars and the film crew were in Royal, helping to make the Blackwood family even more of a sideshow.

Pushing those thoughts aside, he hurried. He needed time to go through her things and look for this special letter his father had sent her. He wanted to see for himself what Buck had had to say. How he explained cutting his own children out of their inheritance.

Kel had never had much of a relationship with his father. Buck had always been too busy swooping down on failing companies to buy them out and sell them, adding to his millions. But none of that mattered now. The family legacy, the ranch, the business, should *stay* in the family. Blackwood Hollow alone was valued at more than $60 million and that wasn't even counting Blackwood Bank and Buck's personal fortune.

Why would he leave it all to Miranda? Hell, they'd been divorced for years. Kel needed to know what was going on and the only way to get those answers was to pry them out of Miranda—even if she didn't know about it.

He opened another door and smiled. Another

Christmas tree stood resplendent in front of the windows overlooking the back of the house and the swimming pool. Women's clothes were strewed across the bed, there was a hairbrush on the dresser and, in spite of the tree, even the air smelled feminine.

In a rush, Kel pushed that thought aside and headed for the closet. It was filled with clothes that he absently noted looked a lot more conservative than what he was used to seeing Miranda wear. He dismissed it when he didn't find anything and went to the bedside tables. Nothing. Then he hit the dresser where he found drawers of sweaters and shirts and yoga pants. Also very un-Miranda-like. No letters, no papers. Nothing.

"Damn it," he muttered, reaching for the next drawer. "Where the hell did she put it?"

He tugged on the drawer pull and saw a collection of delicate bras and panties. Black, pink, red, blue—a rainbow of lace and silk. Gritting his teeth, he ran his hand through the silky fabric, tumbling them all, looking for an envelope that wasn't there. Frustrated, he stopped dead when sounds erupted from the adjoining bathroom. Was she here after all? Was Sophie wrong about Miranda trotting around town spending his father's money in front of an audience of cameras?

The door opened, steam poured out—and through that misty fog, a woman appeared as if from a dream. It wasn't Miranda.

It was the one woman Kel hadn't wanted—or dared—to see again.

Her long strawberry blond hair was damp, lying across her shoulders and draping onto the towel wrapped around what he knew from personal experience was a hell of a body. Her dark green eyes were wide and those long legs of hers were displayed like living temptation.

"Irina Romanov."

She actually tightened her grip on the towel she wore. "Kellan? What are you doing in my room?"

God, that voice. Husky. Tempting. With just the slightest tinge of a Russian accent. In an instant, he was thrown back in time seven years. It had been Christmas then, too. For a week, the two of them had spent nearly every waking moment in bed together. Or anywhere else they'd found a flat surface. And then he'd realized what he was doing and he'd left Texas—and Irina—behind him.

If he allowed it, even now, he could hear her whispers in the dark. Feel her hands on him. Taste her hard nipples as he slammed his body into hers until they were both screaming with need. That long, unforgettable week had seared his soul and stirred a heart he'd believed dead.

Still clutching that too-small towel to her like a shield, Irina looked him dead in the eye and said, "Get out, Kellan."

Probably best, he told himself, since at the moment, all he could think about was tearing that towel off her and tossing her onto the bed. Or the floor.

Or against the wall. His body didn't care how he had her—just that he *did* have her. His dick felt like stone, his breath was caught in his chest and the slow, hard hammer of his heart thundered in his ears.

Kel took a long, deep breath in an attempt to find steadiness. "Fine. I'll go. But I'm not leaving the house. I'll be downstairs when you're dressed."

The minute he left her room, Irina slammed the door and locked it. Turning around, she leaned back against the solid oak panel and rolled her eyes to the ceiling. Her heartbeat was simply out of control, and what felt like dragons were swarming in the pit of her stomach.

She forced air into her lungs and swallowed hard against the rising tide of tears. Why should she cry? She should be outraged. Furious. It had been seven years since he'd walked away, and her first emotion on seeing him again was teary anticipation?

Just like that, the burning in her eyes disappeared and the burn in her heart began. Seeing him again was a shock, even though she'd known he'd come home to Royal after Buck's death. He had to go to his father's funeral after all.

Irina had thought she was prepared—more or less—to see him again. She simply hadn't been ready to greet him while she was stark naked but for a towel. Being naked around Kel was not a good idea. Not with their past. Not with the temptation he presented simply by settling his gaze on her.

He looked good, too. Even better, somehow, than he had so long ago. He wore that elegantly cut suit the way a medieval knight might wear his armor. He was powerful, strong, gorgeous. All things dangerous. His dark brown hair was still kept short—he thought it efficient—and like always, he had a day or two's growth of beard on his face. The scruff of whiskers reminded her of how that stubble alternately tickled and scratched her skin.

The flash in Kel's blue eyes had disarmed her. She had read heat there and remembered the fire that had consumed them both whenever they touched. She remembered long nights, with the Christmas tree lights the only illumination in the room. She remembered lazy dawns, wrapped in each other's arms before she was forced to get up and go to work as a maid in the big house.

In fact, Irina remembered all of it as if that week with him were burned into her brain.

Back then, she'd convinced herself she was living a fairy tale. The oldest son in a dynasty, falling in love with a maid in his father's house. But the fairy tale ended with a whimper when Kellan left Texas. There were no letters, no calls and, apparently, no regrets. Then Irina was alone again with empty dreams and a broken heart.

She'd long suspected Buck had known about what had gone on between her and his oldest son. The older man had been especially kind to her when Kellan left town. And that kindness—like everything else Buck had done for her—was something she could never repay. It had taken her a long time to find her way again and she had no intention of allowing herself to slide back down into darkness. Kellan was here, but wouldn't be for long. Her life was in Royal. Her future was one she would build for herself.

"I don't need Kellan," she said aloud, more to strengthen her resolve than anything. "I've built my own life now. Without him."

Irina wasn't the same woman she had been when she and Kellan were together so briefly—and memorably. She'd been to college. She was in law school now and she was a budding author. She'd grown and taken care of herself and she wouldn't be drawn back into an affair with a man who didn't value her.

It didn't matter that one look at him had undone seven years of self-discipline. She could be strong. All she had to do was keep her distance. A few miles would probably do the trick.

"All right," she said quietly, lifting her chin and squaring her shoulders. "I can do this. Get dressed. Talk to Kellan. And then this time I will be the one to say goodbye."

Two

Lulu Shepard took a good look at Main Street. She wasn't ready to admit this on camera yet, but she actually liked Royal, Texas. The people were nice; their hotel, the Bellamy, was luxurious and the town made a nice change from Manhattan. People were so friendly, too. Not like Manhattan, where you could probably bleed from an artery and go unnoticed.

She hadn't been sure about coming to Royal with Miranda and the rest of the cast of their reality show. But Lulu was really enjoying herself. And she really loved all of the Christmas decorations. Every light pole on the street was wrapped in garland, banners proclaiming Have a Royal Christmas were strung across the street and every tree and shop front was glittering with tiny white lights.

"Afternoon," a tall cowboy with a wicked smile said as he passed, tipping his hat.

"Well, helloooo." Lulu turned to admire the man from the rear and had to admit that view was pretty good, too.

Oh, there were so many delicious opportunities to get into a little trouble while they were in Royal. If she and Serafina couldn't find a way to shake this town up a little, then Lulu didn't know who could.

She wore a black knit tunic sweater with black tights and black ankle boots with a three-inch heel. Her bright red overcoat swung around her knees with every step and she grinned for no particular reason.

"There's just something about a small town, don't you think, Fee?"

Her best friend, Seraphina Martinez, whirled around, letting her long forest green coat swing in the wind. She, too, was wearing New York black, but for her coat. Her long brown hair was perfectly styled and lifted in the wind. Her brown eyes were shining when she smiled. "You know, I didn't think I'd like it, but I do. It's sort of like a movie set—only real." Then she sent a glance at the camera crew following them. "Come on, guys, we've got some shopping to do. Let's show America how small-town Texas lives."

Lulu laughed and fell into line behind her friend and the other members of the *Secret Lives of NYC*

Ex-Wives cast. Zooey Kostas, sweet and vulnerable, was always on the lookout for her next ex. Rafaela Marchesi was never afraid to toss one of her friends under the bus as long as it earned her a few more minutes of screen time. Then there was Seraphina, the take-charge woman in their little group. Fee had a great laugh and a huge heart. And Miranda was the last—sort of a mother-bear kind of woman, which didn't earn her a lot of time on the show, since as their producer was forever saying, "Scandal sells."

But when Miranda DuPree had announced she was coming to Royal for a funeral, the powers that be at the network had decided it would be a great idea for the whole cast to go along.

Though she liked Miranda a lot, Lulu hadn't thought much of the idea at first. Now she couldn't imagine why. An icy wind lifted a lock of her thick black hair and tossed it across her eyes. She plucked it free, grinned and hurried her steps to catch up with Fee. There were so many new and interesting shops waiting.

Kellan had one hand planted on the mantel and was staring at a blazing fire in the stone hearth when he heard her come into the room. Hell, she moved so quietly maybe he had just *sensed* her.

He turned to face her and his breath caught in his chest. Seven years since he'd last seen her and every cell in his body was responding to her presence. Time, it seemed, hadn't cooled off what he felt for her. Damn it.

"What are you doing here, Kellan?"

That voice tugged at his insides and awakened even more memories that had been asleep until that moment. Not good. He'd once walked away from her because he felt he had to. He'd had nothing to offer her then and nothing had changed since. He had to stay cool, keep his distance.

But she was looking at him with a carefully banked fury he'd never seen before. And for some damn reason, that put him on the defensive.

"This is still *Blackwood Hollow*," he said tightly. "I'm a Blackwood. I don't have to explain why I'm in the house I grew up in."

"You don't live here anymore," she reminded him.

Tipping his head to one side, he narrowed his gaze on her. "Yeah. But I didn't know you were still living here."

"Not surprising," she pointed out. "You haven't been back in this house for seven years."

A jab, well aimed. Kellan had avoided this house like it was haunted. And maybe, he thought now, it *was*. Ghosts of his childhood, memories of his mother. But mostly, it was the memories of his week with Irina that plagued him. Being in this house made those ghostly images in his mind more real. More corporeal. As if he could reach out and touch them, bring back those moments in time to relive at his leisure.

His gaze swept her up and down in a blink of an eye, taking in everything, missing nothing. Her long, wavy hair was still damp, but now she wore a loose-fitting yellow jersey shirt with a neckline wide enough to bare her shoulders. At five feet ten inches tall, Irina had legs that were long and shapely, though at the moment they were covered by a pair of gray yoga pants that clung to every inch. Black ballet flats were on her feet.

Kellan's whole body tensed.

Even dressed casually, Irina was more beautiful than any other woman would have been decked out in diamonds. Heat rushed through him. The sparks in her eyes intrigued him. There was a pride and a self-confidence about her now and he liked it. Irina had once told him that in Russia, she'd been a model, but when he'd known her, she'd been shy, unsure of herself. As if she were lost and hadn't been able to find her way.

This Irina, strong enough to meet his gaze and lift her chin in defiance, was someone new, and damned if she wasn't even more attractive.

She crossed her arms over her chest, unconsciously lifting her breasts, making his mouth go dry. "What were you doing in my room? Going through my things?"

"Didn't know that was your room," he said shortly. "I thought it was Miranda's."

One of her expertly shaped eyebrows lifted and he knew what she was thinking.

"God, no." He shuddered at the idea of sex with his late father's ex. Even if it hadn't been more than a little gross to contemplate sex with his father's former lover, he wouldn't have been interested in Miranda. She was too...practiced at seduction. "Trust me," he said. "It's not that."

"All right." Her arms dropped to her sides. "Then why were you looking for her room?"

He took a deep breath and gritted his teeth. Kellan wasn't used to explaining himself. Mostly, he did what he wanted when he wanted and screw whoever didn't like it. Made life easier. Back in the day, Irina never would have confronted him like this. And maybe that was why he was willing to answer her. Damned if he didn't admire the fire in her eyes. "For something to explain why Buck did what he did. They read his will today and dear old Dad left her *everything*."

"Yes, I know. Kace told me earlier today when he came to tell me about the inheritance Buckley left to me."

Surprise had him speechless for a moment. Kellan never would have imagined Buckley Blackwood even *noticing* a maid in his house, let alone naming her in his will. Buck hadn't been exactly known for being a kind soul. He had marched through his life, single-mindedly focused on his business, his fortune.

Finally, he recovered enough to ask, "My father left you something?"

"Is it really so shocking? Your father was very good to me."

"I know you always thought so." He shook his

head as if denying what he was saying. "But Buck was never described as *generous*."

"Fine. Think that if it comforts you."

"Comforts me?" Kellan stared at her for a long minute. "What the hell does that mean?"

"Never mind." Irina swung her long hair back over her shoulder and her shirt dipped just a bit lower over her upper arm. "You've obviously set your mind on who you believe your father was. I can't change your mind."

Maybe Buck was good to Irina, but Kellan couldn't be budged from his own perspective on his father. Hell, he'd lived it, hadn't he?

"But you haven't answered me. Why did you want to look through Miranda's things?"

Hard to keep his mind on business when he was fantasizing about sliding that shirt all the way off, then—"I heard Buck sent her a letter. I want to see it. Need to know what's in it."

"It's none of your business."

"Of course it's my business," he snapped and rubbed one hand across the back of his neck. "I need to know what she knows. I need to understand why Buck left her everything."

For a long moment, Irina just watched him, and the steady stare from her dark green eyes made him uneasy. For good reason, as it turned out.

"No. I can't help you, Kellan. And I won't let you spy on Miranda."

Irritation flared to life inside him. "You can't stop me."

"I can tell her what you did."

"Letting her know after the fact won't change anything," he said quickly.

Even though she was standing between him and what he needed to do, he couldn't help thinking that it was damned good to see her again. *Too* good. He should have been past this, Kellan told himself.

He'd stayed away from her deliberately for years, because being close to her and not having her would have killed him. Hell, she was *part* of the reason he'd moved to Nashville. But even distance from her hadn't been enough to wipe away the memory of her. She'd still been with him. In his dreams. In those quiet, waking moments when he didn't have enough to occupy his thoughts.

And every time she popped into his mind—way too often—he shut it down fast. He spent empty nights with other women telling himself that sex with them was just as good as it had been with Irina. Lies he wanted to believe because they made it all that much easier.

But standing here, with her just out of arm's reach, those lies rushed back to bite him in the ass. So naturally, he buried what he was feeling beneath the anger still riding him since the will reading.

"Since when are you Miranda's friend?" he asked. "You're really ready to stand with her against me?"

"And how do I owe loyalty to you? You disappeared, Kellan."

"I had to."

"Yes, I'm sure." She entered the room but walked

a wide path around him to do it. She dropped onto a corner of the couch, curled her legs up beneath her and tipped her head to one side to look up at him. "She's Buck's guest."

"Buck's dead."

Emotion flashed briefly in her eyes. "I know. But this is his home—"

"And mine," he added.

"Not for years," she reminded him. "You walked away, Kellan. From your home. From your family. From Buck. From *me*."

And there it was. The past was in the room with them, with its hungry, snapping jaws, not really caring whom it bit into, just wanting the pain. The blood.

He'd known that the minute they saw each other again, they'd have to relive this. He'd have to look at old decisions and would be forced to defend them. He didn't know that he could.

"I had to leave." He shoved his hands into his pockets.

Irina looked up at the man around whom she'd once built ridiculous dreams. The oldest son of the man she'd worked for—the man she owed so much. Buck had rescued her. Given her a chance she might never have had otherwise. She'd come to this house broken, to work as a maid, to go to school, to rebuild a life that had been shattered.

Kellan was the man who had touched her in so many ways, he'd left her breathless. She'd trusted him, in spite of everything she'd already been through. She'd believed in him when she shouldn't have. And then, he'd simply *left her*.

Seven years ago, they'd had a week together. He'd been wounded. She'd been hurt. And yet, somehow, for that one week, they'd reached beyond themselves and found something she had believed was magical. Stolen time, stolen passion and her silly dreams of something more. Then it was over and she was broken again.

Irina wouldn't let it happen this time. Wouldn't let her heart overrun her mind. But even as she thought it, she knew that the reason she'd dropped onto the brown leather sofa was because Kellan still made her legs weak. Her heartbeat was racing and there were tingles of expectation, anticipation, at the core of her. It seemed her body didn't care what her mind had to say. It only wanted.

Irina looked up at him and deliberately hid everything she was feeling.

"Yes, you had to leave. You said as much to me. Seven years ago." The leather felt cold and that chill was seeping inside her. "You said a lot of things. I remember."

Kellan nodded. "Yeah, I do, too. I didn't want to hurt you, Irina."

Her gaze locked on him and she drew a long, shallow breath. Irina didn't want to talk about any of it, either. Didn't want to remember the sound of his voice saying, *I can't be what you want.* Or, *This isn't real, Irina. It can't be. I won't let it be.* So she swallowed hard and hid what she was feeling. "You may not have wanted to, but you did. Still, that's not why you're here now, is it?"

"No," he said, inclining his head slightly. "It's not." He braced his feed wide apart, as if preparing for a battle. "Tell me this. How long is Miranda staying in Royal?"

She shrugged as if indifferent. "I don't really know. She's made no plans to leave as far as I know."

"Of course she hasn't," he muttered, pushing one hand through his short, neat hair. "Why would she? Has the run of this house, all the money Buck left her and plenty of time to cause more trouble."

Miranda had always seemed like a nice woman to Irina. In fact, they'd bonded some over a shared past of heartbreak and mistrust. And seeing how Buck's grown children had treated Miranda had guaranteed that Irina would stand up for her. Since she'd once been an underdog herself, she would always stand up for people she thought were being bullied.

"What exactly, apart from her marrying and divorcing your father," Irina asked, "do you have against her?"

"Isn't that enough?"

"No." Love died. Marriages ended. She'd lived it herself and usually there was more than one person to blame for it.

"It is for me," he countered. "She's got no rights here as far as I'm concerned."

Shaking her head, Irina watched him. "Then it's good it's not up to you."

"What the hell, Irina? I don't understand this," he admitted. "You were always more loyal to Buck than he deserved, so why would you switch that loyalty to Miranda?"

"And you were always harder on Buck than he deserved. Your father was more than you think he was."

"I don't believe it," he snapped. "And that doesn't answer the question. Why are you being so damn protective of Miranda of all people?"

Because, Irina thought, she understood Buck's ex-wife. She knew what it was to be called a gold digger. Knew what it was to love and lose. Knew how hard it was to start over. To rebuild your life. How could Irina not stand by Miranda, when Buck had stood by her?

"It was your father's fortune to do with as he pleased. Why do you get to say that he can't leave Miranda everything?" Forcing herself to her feet, Irina locked her traitorous knees so they wouldn't wobble on her again and tipped her head back to stare up at him. Looking into those lake-blue eyes of his sent tendrils of heat spiraling through her, but Irina did her best to ignore them. "I *am* being loyal to Buck. To his wishes."

He slowly shook his head and watched her curiously. "What the hell did he ever do for you?"

Everything, she thought but didn't say. Buckley Blackwood had played guardian angel to a lot of people and he'd insisted on remaining anonymous. So no one—not even his children—knew what a good man he really had been. But Irina would never forget.

"That's none of your business, Kellan. You walked away. You don't get to show up seven years later and demand answers to anything."

He huffed out a breath and took a step closer. Irina steeled herself because she could smell his cologne. That same wild, spicy scent that seemed to chase her through sleepless nights. His jaw was clenched, his eyes snapping with sparks of frustration, and tension practically radiated from him in thick waves.

She felt that same tension pulsing inside her and she hated it. He'd once had so much power over her. One look from him turned her body into a molten puddle of need. One touch and she was burning. Orgasms with Kellan were more than she would have thought possible.

But strangely, what she missed most was lying in the circle of his arms, darkness all around them, while they talked and laughed together. That closeness, that intimacy, had meant everything to her and had hurt her the most when it was gone.

"I used to admire that hard head of yours," he said, his voice lower, more intimate.

Now it was more than her knees that were feeling weak. Everything in her yearned. A slow burn started deep inside and bubbled in her bloodstream. This was dangerous. A temptation to go back rather than forward. She'd fought hard to reclaim her life, her heart, her mind after Kellan left. Irina couldn't let herself be swept into another temporary liaison. And with Kellan, she knew it would be nothing *but* temporary.

"Kellan..." Warning? Invitation? Even Irina didn't know for sure.

"You're still so damn beautiful," he murmured.

And he was still enticing.

"I think I'm going to kiss you," he said, one eyebrow quirking. "Do you have a problem with that?"

Say yes. Say yes. Say yes.

"No," she whispered.

So he did and the first touch of his lips to hers set that slow burn free and turned it into a wildfire deep within her body. She remembered that fire so well. She welcomed the flames, though she knew she shouldn't. Irina was helpless to stop herself. Kellan had always had this effect on her and seven years hadn't changed a thing.

His hands came down onto her shoulders and pulled her toward him. She kept her mouth on his as her arms snaked around his waist. The feel of him pressed against her made her body ache. An aching, molten heat settled in her core and left her hungry for so much more than a kiss.

His tongue swept into her mouth and tangled with hers. She tightened her hold on him, and met him stroke for stroke, need for need. The kiss awakened her from a years-long sleep and the awakening was almost painful. Her body hummed with anticipation. Her mind clouded over with too many sensations rising and falling to make sense of any of them.

Her breath caught in her chest as she gave herself up to the wonder of the fire even while a small voice within shouted at her to be careful. To step back. To remember that though his touch was magical, he wasn't staying this time, either.

And that thought was finally enough to penetrate the fog in her brain. To push past what he made her feel long enough that she could remind herself that only pain waited for her if she let this go on.

Irina pulled back, shaking her head as much to convince herself as him. She took a deep breath to steady herself and met his gaze, no matter what it cost her to look into those blue eyes again. "We shouldn't have done that."

He scrubbed one hand across his face, then the back of his neck. His breath came hard and fast so she knew he'd been as affected as she had been. Small comfort, she supposed.

Nodding, he said, "Right. Mistake." His gaze locked on hers, he added, "A good one."

Her stomach jumped. "No, it wasn't."

"Liar."

Her heart jittered.

"Fine. It felt good. But then, chemistry was never our problem," she said, remembering. God, how she remembered what happened when they were together.

"No. It wasn't." He stepped back from her as if he didn't quite trust himself not to reach for her again.

And Irina didn't know if she was sad about that or grateful.

"I couldn't stay back then, Irina," he was saying. "There were too many memories in Royal. Too much pain."

She knew that. He'd lost his wife a year before he and Irina got together. So he'd come to her, a widower with a broken heart and a shattered soul, and for a very short while, they'd healed each other.

"So you left and shared the pain."

His head snapped up and his gaze fixed on hers. "That wasn't my intention."

"And yet it's what you did."

Clearly irritated, he pushed one hand through his hair. "I didn't come here tonight to argue with you."

"No," she said. "You came here to spy on Miranda."

"I want answers," he countered.

"Get them another way."

A muscle in his jaw ticked. "I hope Miranda appreciates how you're defending her."

"I'm not doing this for her," Irina said. "Or not just for her. I'm doing this mainly for your father. Buck wrote his will. It laid out *his* wishes. Kellan, you don't get to disregard them simply because you don't like them."

"Man, I hope Buck appreciated the tiger he had defending him."

A small smile curved her mouth briefly. "He did."

Nodding, Kellan studied her for a long minute. "I'm not going to let this go."

"I didn't think you would," she said. "But you

should. And, Kellan, you should know that Buck loved you. Loved all of you."

"Please." He snorted dismissively and waved one hand at her as if erasing her words entirely.

"He did."

"And he proved that by leaving our family legacy to a woman he chose to not stay married to?"

"I don't know why he did that," Irina admitted. "But I always trusted Buck."

"There's the difference between us, then," Kellan said softly, his gaze locked with hers. "I never trusted my father. And I won't start now."

"So you're not going back to Nashville?" She had hoped that after the funeral and the reading of the will that Kellan would once again leave Royal.

"Not a chance," he promised. "I'm not going anywhere until this whole situation is settled." He turned on his heel and headed for the front door. He paused only briefly to look back at her. When their eyes met, he said, "You haven't seen the last of me, Irina."

That sounded like a promise, too, and she hated that she was pleased by it.

"How'd the big spy operation go?"

Kellan glanced over his shoulder at his younger brother as Vaughn walked into the great room and dropped onto the closest sofa. Since Vaughn lived in Dallas now, he was staying at their mother's friend Dixie's ranch, Magnolia Acres. Since Kellan was in Royal for a while, though, Vaughn was dropping in and out. It was good to spend real time with his brother and sister instead of the quick visits he usually made. The only time Kellan stayed at his ranch himself was when he came back to Royal to see his brother and sister. Now he was rethinking the whole drop-in-anytime thing.

Scowling, Kellan said, "As well as you said it would."

Vaughn laughed shortly. "It was a crappy plan, Kel. Face it. Storm Dad's house, snoop through Miranda's stuff?"

Kellan stalked to the wet bar in the corner of the room. Bending down, he opened the fridge and grabbed a beer. "You want one?"

"Hell yes."

Kellan crossed the room again, handed a beer to his brother and then took a seat opposite him. "I never got to go through her things. Irina was there and stopped me."

Vaughn's eyebrows lifted. "Interesting," he mused. "I didn't know anyone *could* stop you once you had your decision made."

Kellan took a swig of beer and avoided looking at Vaughn. His brother was entirely too perceptive. "Doesn't matter."

"Uh-huh. So, how's Irina?"

Now he did fire a hard look at his brother. "She's fine."

"Better than fine, if you ask me," Vaughn said with a small smile. "We both saw her at the service, and gotta say, she's still hot."

"Hot?"

"I'm not blind, Kel. Even if you are."

"I'm not blind, either," he snapped and took another hard pull of his beer.

"Good to know." Vaughn sat up and braced his elbows on his knees. "So you going to do anything about it?"

The taste of Irina rose up in his mind. The feel of her body pressed to his. Her breath on his cheek. The scent of her hair. The silk of her skin. He took another drink of his beer and let the icy brew dampen the fires inside. He really didn't need his brother poking at him over Irina when his own mind and body were doing just fine on that front. "What the hell, Vaughn?"

He held up one hand. "Fine. I'll back off."

"Thank you."

"But," he added, and Kellan frowned at him, "all those years ago, you two had something."

"How do you know?"

"Everybody knew."

So much for a secret affair. "It was a long time ago."

"True. But according to gossip and our baby sister, Irina's still single. So are you."

Kellan's gaze narrowed. "I'm not looking, Vaughn."

"Because of Shea?" Vaughn's voice was a whisper.

Kellan shot off the couch like he was on a spring. It had been eight years since his wife had died in that car accident. Eight years and he still didn't want to think about that day. Remember the staggering loss. Remember that touching Irina only a year after that loss had made him feel like a damn cheat. "Don't talk about her."

"A lot of rules," his brother said softly. "No talk of Irina. Shea, either. What am I allowed to say to you?"

"How about good-night?" Kellan snapped. "Or even better, *I'm headed back to Magnolia Acres*. Or even better, Dallas."

Vaughn laughed. "Yeah, not happening. I'm here for a couple more days. Have some friends I want to see while I'm in Royal. Now that the services and the will reading are done, I'm free."

"Why are you not pissed?" Kellan demanded suddenly. "About Dad leaving everything to Miranda? Why isn't that burning your ass?"

Vaughn's features smoothed out into a blank slate. Only his eyes flashed to let Kellan know he wasn't as disinterested as he was pretending to be. "Because I don't want Buck's money. I made my own way with no help from our father. It's too damn late for him to do anything for me. So let Miranda have it. I hope she chokes on it."

"I call bull." Kellan pointed his beer at Vaughn. "Maybe you don't want the money, but I know losing Blackwood Hollow to that woman has to be eating at you. That's *family land*, Vaughn. It's our land. Our ranch. Our damned legacy."

Studying his own beer, Vaughn was silent for a long minute or two. Finally, though, he said, "Being pissed won't change anything, Kel. So accept the fact that our dad was a dick and move the hell on already."

"No."

Vaughn gave another short laugh and lifted his beer in a toast. "Fine. You go ahead. Charge into the dragon's den and try to come out with the magic sword or whatever. But don't expect me to help you do it."

Kellan said, "Just don't get in my way."

"Deal." Vaughn turned for the door. "Now, I'm going to Dixie's place. I'm too tired to keep jousting with you. Good luck on your next caper, 007."

Life, Kellan thought, might have been a lot easier if he'd been an only child.

The next morning, Kellan was working at his ranch, wearing some jeans, a dark green flannel shirt and a heavy brown leather jacket. His old boots were scuffed and worn, and stepping into them made him feel complete somehow. You could take a man off the ranch, dress him in a suit and toss him into a city, but it seemed you couldn't take the Texas out of him.

He was tired, though. The argument with Vaughn bothered him, but it was that kiss with Irina that had kept him awake most of the night. He'd played it over and over in his head for hours, like a damn movie on constant rewind and replay. He hadn't been able to turn it off. To ignore what seeing her again, touching her again, had done to his body. So a night of self-imposed torture left him squinting into the early-morning sunlight and wishing for more coffee.

Standing on the wide front porch in the cold, blustery wind, he scanned the property he'd purchased five years ago. He should probably rent it out, but the truth was, it was nice to have his own place to stay in when he was in Royal. He had a great foreman, who took care of the place while Kellan lived in Nashville, and, as an investment, the ranch couldn't be better. The land itself was worth almost twice as much as it had been when he'd bought it and that wasn't even counting the value of the palatial ranch house and outbuildings. Not to mention the stock—thousands of heads of cattle and horses.

But he hadn't bought it for its financial worth. Instead, it was a touchstone of sorts. A reminder that though staying in Royal had been too much for him seven years ago, this corner of Texas was still his home. His roots ran deep here. The Blackwoods had been in this area for more than a hundred years.

Which was just one more reason why he wasn't about to give up his family legacy to a gold digger. Just the thought of Miranda DuPree made his hackles rise and had him grinding his teeth together so hard, he was half-surprised they didn't shatter. He'd thought Miranda was out of their lives when she and Buck divorced—and now she was back, worse than ever. "What the hell was Buck thinking?"

When a bright red Jeep zipped up the drive and came to a screeching halt almost directly in front of him, Kellan smiled in spite of the dark thoughts tumbling through his mind. His baby sister hopped out of the car and shivered in the cold wind.

"Hi, Kel," Sophie said as she tugged her black jacket tighter around her.

People didn't usually think of Texas as cold-weather country. But winters could be harsh and even though snow was rare, the icy wind could cut like a knife.

"What're you doing here so early?"

She waved one hand, smiled, and Kellan realized what a beauty his sister had become. Just an inch or so shorter than Irina, Sophie had long auburn hair, brown eyes and a curvy body that Kellan really didn't want to acknowledge. As far as he was concerned, there was no man good enough for Sophie—so she should just be alone. If they were Catholic, he'd be voting for a convent.

"I've got a ten o'clock appointment at the Courtyard. My client wants to look at the antiques at Priceless."

Sophie, at only twenty-seven, ran a popular YouTube channel on style, was a licensed interior decorator and had her own shop in Royal. And as a designer, of course she would love shopping at the Courtyard. The place had grown from a single re-habbed barn housing antiques into a series of eclectic businesses, including a few artisans and cafés.

"I saw Vaughn at the diner having coffee and he told me you'd be up and moving because when he left here last night, you were too wired to sleep."

"Our brother's got a big mouth," Kellan muttered. "What's up, Sophie?"

She sighed and flipped her hair out of her face when the wind gusted. "I couldn't sleep last night, either. I kept thinking about the will and Miranda and us, and I guess I just wanted to talk to you. See what you think about all of it."

He scowled and tugged his hat down firmer on his head. "I think I'm going to be going into town to talk to Kace later today. See if I can find a way to fight this will."

"Okay, but what if he says there isn't one?"

"Then we fight anyway," Kellan said tightly. "Damned if we just hand over our home to Miranda."

She nodded and smiled. "Okay, good. Because I was thinking maybe I could snoop around a little. Talk to people. See if anyone knows anything about Miranda. Gossip in Royal lives forever. Plus, I know Miranda's come back to town more than a few times since the divorce. I mean, you and Vaughn and I, we haven't really been spending any time at the house in years."

True. They'd all avoided the house because they were busy avoiding Buck. Kellan lived in Nashville now, Sophie had her own house in Pine Valley and Vaughn was in Dallas these days.

"Maybe," she continued, "there's a reason behind Dad doing this to us. And maybe I can help find it."

Three

Kellan looked into her eyes and saw the worry and the hurt there, and if he could, he would have reached beyond the grave to grab his father and curse him for giving Sophie pain. He knew she wanted to help him find answers and, hell, maybe she could. Women talked more easily to other women. If she could pry some secrets loose, it might give them something to use against Miranda.

"Sounds good," he said and saw the flash of pleasure in her eyes. "Where are you going to start?"

"After my appointment, I thought I'd go to the ranch and talk to Irina."

"No." The one word shot from him before he could hold it back.

"Why not?"

Good question. The answer wasn't something he wanted to share. Kellan didn't want to risk his sister and his former lover having a private chat. God knows what Irina would have to say about him. He certainly hadn't given her any reason to speak well about him.

"I'm going to the house later today." That hadn't been the plan, but plans change. "So I'll take care of talking to Irina. Why don't you speak to some of Miranda's friends in town? Maybe some of the women she dragged here with her from New York."

Sophie frowned thoughtfully. "That's probably a good idea. I mean, she went to New York after the divorce, she probably had plenty to say about Dad when their breakup was fresh."

It actually was a good idea. Then he had another one. If their little sister talked to Vaughn about all of this, maybe he'd change his mind. "Okay, then. And why don't you give Vaughn a call? Tell him what we're up to."

"Oh, he won't be interested." Sophie shrugged. "Soon enough, he'll be back in Dallas running his company. He said he doesn't give a damn what Miranda does with her inheritance. It has nothing to do with him."

So much for that. In a way, Kel understood the attitude. His brother had built his own fortune at Blackwood Energy Corp., so he didn't need Buck's money. But hell, neither did Kel. It was the damn principle of the thing that motivated Kellan. And he wished Vaughn would stick around long enough to stand with his siblings.

"Okay, then, for now, it's you and me, baby sister." He reached out with one arm and pulled her into a hug. She held him tight, then let go.

"I'll let you know if I find out anything and you tell me if Irina has anything to say, okay?"

"Sure." Nodding, he watched her hop back into her car. "And drive slower, will you?"

"Nope!" She grinned, slammed the door and gunned the engine. Whipping the red car around, she peeled off down the drive, leaving a fan of spun gravel in her wake.

"Damn it." Sophie always drove too fast. As a teenager, she'd had her license pulled first by Buck and then by Sheriff Battle. And that hadn't stopped her. The last time Kellan had been in town, Nathan Battle had told him that Sophie's speeding tickets alone were paying for the remodel of the sheriff's station.

Pushing that thought out of his mind, Kellan headed for the stables. What he needed was some hard work. Work that would keep his hands busy and free his mind to think about what his next step would be.

Though he already knew the answer.

He had to see Irina again.

"I'm meeting my friends in Royal for lunch," Miranda said. "I've told them all about the Royal Diner

for years and now they want to try it out in person.
Would you like to join us?"

Miranda had been in Royal since a couple of days
before the will reading, and in that time she and Irina
had become friends. When Miranda was still married
to Buck, the two women hadn't really bonded. Irina
was more shy back then, too. Less sure of herself.
They actually had more in common than she would
have thought. They were both divorced—though their
situations were wildly different. They were both re-
building their lives. And they both knew hidden
truths about Buckley Blackwood. Each of them, in
their own ways, owed Buck a lot.

It was good to be able to talk about the older man
with someone who understood. Almost no one in
Royal knew the real Buck.

In business, Buck had been ruthless, determined
and unstoppable. But in private, the man had helped
more people than anyone would guess. It really irritated Irina that his own children were clueless about
that side of Buck. But she'd once promised him that
she'd keep his secrets. Just because he was dead
didn't give her permission to talk. Did it?

"Thank you, Miranda," she said. "I really appreciate it. But I think I'm going to work on my book
this morning. I'd like to finish the chapter at least."

She was so close to finishing the book she'd been
driven to write. Her own personal background story
was one she thought a lot of women could connect
to. Maybe not the particulars of her experience,
but the spirit of the story. Picking yourself up and

starting over would be a clarion call to those who might be feeling hopeless.

And an agent and a publisher had believed in her, too. She'd sold her book six months ago and it was still a thrill to her. Soon, she'd be a published author and then an immigration lawyer, and her own American dream story would be complete.

Or as complete as it could be without the man she'd once believed to be the love of her life.

Miranda smiled and nodded. "I get it. And I know Buck was proud of you for everything you've accomplished."

"Thank you," she said. "That means a lot."

"And," Miranda added as she picked up her bag, "if you're willing, I'd love to read some of your book."

Irina almost choked. She hadn't expected that rush of wild panic. Someone wanted to read what she'd written? Why was that terrifying? Soon it would be out on shelves and hopefully a lot of people would want to read it. But this was different. This was someone she *knew*. Yes, she'd submitted it to an agent and publisher, but that was business. Letting someone she knew and liked read it was something different.

Miranda laughed. "Okay, never mind. I can see how unnerved you are at the idea."

"No," Irina said, taking a step forward as she got a firm grip on the swirls of what felt like eagles in her stomach. Then she sighed. "All right, yes, I'm a little nervous at the thought. But I really would love for you to read the first chapter and tell me what you think."

It sounded terrifying, of course. But one day soon, everyone in Royal would see it, buy it, read it. It might be a good thing to get an idea of what people would think ahead of time.

"Great!" Miranda gave her a quick hug. "I'm sure it's wonderful, so don't look so worried."

Irina laughed a little. "I think worrying is what I do best."

Smiling, Miranda said, "I'll see you tonight. And remember, you're not a maid here anymore, Irina. You're a guest."

Technically. But Miranda now owned the lovely house and Irina was Buck's guest, not hers. So she would pitch in and help out as much as she could.

"Thank you. I appreciate that." She gave a look around the great room, with its plush but homey atmosphere, and at the Christmas tree, which she personally decorated every year. "But I've worked here for more than seven years now. While I'm here, I'll continue to help the housekeeper."

Miranda studied her for a long moment. "I get that. You don't want to be beholden to anyone. You need to steer your own path. Pay your own way."

"Yes," Irina said.

"You know, I think you and I are very much alike."

Irina smiled. She'd had the same thought. "Have a good time."

"Right." Miranda headed for the front door. "I'll see you later."

Alone, Irina thought about their conversation. About the secrets she held. About promises made and about Kellan, still holding so much anger for his late father. And she made a decision.

Working on the book would have to wait. First, she had to see Kellan. Tell him things he should know.

The diner was kitschy, with the decor set firmly in the fifties—black-and-white tile floor, red faux leather booths and an actual jukebox on one wall. Lulu was charmed. The waitresses seemed to know everyone in there and the camera crew following Lulu and her friends didn't intimidate anyone. Instead, the locals were interested, excited even.

Except for one man.

Of course, he was gorgeous. His brown eyes were flashing with irritation and his rumpled dark brown hair was a little too long. The collar of his dress shirt was unbuttoned and his dark red tie loosened. He had a sheaf of papers spread out over the table in front of him and a cup of coffee at his elbow. The hostile looks he was shooting everyone involved in her reality show left no doubt what he thought of any of them.

Well, if he wanted privacy to work, Lulu told herself, he shouldn't have come to a diner. The scowl on his face seemed to be a permanent fixture and she wondered idly why she found that appealing. A man that inherently cranky shouldn't be so attractive. But he certainly was. He sipped his coffee, made a note on one of the papers and then frowned again at her group and the camera crew.

Fee and the rest of the girls were oblivious, joking together about another day of shopping or perhaps a spa day at the Bellamy, where they were all staying. But Lulu couldn't stop watching *him*. So she was aware when Miranda came into the diner and stopped at his table. Briefly, the scowl on his face lifted and she wondered how Miranda had managed that small miracle. While they talked, Lulu scooted out of the booth and walked up to join them. She heard her friend saying something about Buck's will, but she missed the context because both people got quiet as soon as she arrived.

"Hi, Miranda." She smiled at her friend, then sent a deliberate wink at the crabby man frowning at her.

"Lulu!" Miranda gave her a hug and grinned. "Did you guys have another fabulous morning of shopping?"

"We did. It was wonderful. We went back to the Courtyard shops." They'd all enjoyed it so much the day before, they'd returned to hit the stores they'd missed on their first visit.

"And your camera crew loved it, too?" the man asked snidely, inserting himself into the conversation. "Get every little purchase covered, did they? Want to make sure America sees you spending your exes' money."

"I'm sorry?" she asked, pointedly meeting his less-than-friendly stare.

"That would be nice, but I doubt you are," he said.

"Um," Miranda interrupted, confusion written plainly on her features. "Lulu Shepard, this is my ex-husband's lawyer, Kace LeBlanc. Kace, Lulu."

"A lawyer," Lulu said with feigned, over-the-top sorrow. "That explains it."

His eyes flashed. "What does that mean?"

She shrugged and ignored Miranda's growing confusion to continue the byplay with Kace. "I've rarely met a lawyer with a measurable sense of humor or any talent for finding joy in life."

"Is that right? Well, my *joy in life* isn't dependent on the presence of a camera."

Their cameramen, Henry and Sam, maneuvered into position so they could capture this whole scene. The guys were experts at this and there was nothing that sold better on film than conflict. They were probably sensing a good one right here and they weren't wrong. But Lulu didn't care. She was starting to enjoy herself.

She tossed her hair back over her shoulder. "What do you like about your job, then? Evicting widows and orphans?"

Henry snorted a muffled laugh.

Miranda said, "Now, Lulu…"

Miranda was always the most altruistic of the Exes. The one who looked out for everyone else. She hated an argument; that was why she was the peacemaker on their show. Lulu sort of liked arguments. Especially when she was trading barbs with a gorgeous man with the most beautiful brown eyes she'd ever seen.

"Seriously?" Kace demanded. "That's the best you've got?" He pushed out of the booth and stood much taller than her, even with her three-inch heels.

"Oh no," Lulu assured him, a small smile curving her mouth. "I can do way better. I promise you. I'm just getting started."

"Ah." He nodded sagely and waved one hand to indicate Henry and Sam. "Had to wait for the cameras to get set. Have they caught your 'good side'?"

"Every side is my good side," she quipped and stared up at him.

He met her gaze and she saw a flash of interest spark in those amazing eyes of his before he said, "Is there some reason you have to have cameras in the diner? Do you guys eat with your feet? Do they need to document you chewing?"

"It's a reality show," Lulu reminded him. "They follow us around. And they probably want to catch some local color in Royal—which you're currently providing. And no one but you seems to have a problem with it."

"Everyone else is too polite to say anything."

"Um…" Miranda's voice slid into the fray but couldn't stop it.

"But polite doesn't occur to you, does it?"

"I'm too busy for social niceties."

"So busy you have to work in a diner?" Lulu countered, really starting to enjoy herself now. He was angry, and that put a fire in his brown eyes that was both magnetic and irritating. "Where's your office? Over a dry cleaner's?"

His mouth worked, then tightened into a grim slash. "My office is being painted. I came here to get some work done, which would be easier if you and your fellow 'actors' weren't making so damn much noise."

"Um, maybe..." Miranda's voice was barely noticed.

"Not actors," Lulu told him. "Just people. Reality show, remember? Do you have memory problems?"

"Oh," he said, glaring down at her, "there's a problem in here, but it's not with my memory."

"Well, you'd think a lawyer would know that a diner wasn't going to give him quiet. Why don't you go to the library?"

"It was fine in here until your crowd showed up."

"Okay, let's just leave it there, all right?" Miranda took Lulu's arm, clearly ready to drag her away. But Lulu wasn't ready just yet. Honestly, she'd wanted to meet the gorgeous, cranky man, but she hadn't expected such explosive chemistry between them. Everyone in the diner was watching them and she had no doubt the cameras had caught the entire exchange between her and Kace LeBlanc. Kace. What a great name.

"We'll let you work, then," Lulu said as he sat down again. "Be sure to tell us if we're too loud, though. Not that we'll get quiet, but I don't want to miss you being annoyed."

His lips quirked briefly. "I don't imagine you're ever quiet."

She gave him a brief, sly smile in return. "Nope. And in certain situations I've been known to scream."

Later that afternoon, Irina pulled up to Kellan's ranch and parked outside the main house.

With the engine off, she simply sat there and studied the place. Two stories, sparkling white with black shutters and black newel posts on the wide wraparound porch. Oaks surrounded the building, offering shade in the summer and stark definition in winter.

It wasn't the first time she'd been there. Since Kellan left Royal for Nashville, she'd been here several times. Well, not *inside*, but she'd driven past it. Parked outside it. Not obsessively or anything. But the ranch had become a touchstone of sorts. The last piece of Kellan to remain in Texas. She could tell herself he hadn't left entirely. And indeed, she knew that he came back from time to time to see his brother and sister. And to check in on his own property.

But he'd *avoided* Irina.

Knowing that had stung her deeply. But she'd gotten past it. She'd focused on work. On school. On building a future for herself. Now she didn't think of him every day anymore. She didn't dream of him every night. But when she did, it was with an ache of remembered loss that was so strong, sometimes she woke up crying. And that infuriated her. Why should she cry for a man who hadn't wanted her? Why should she give her tears to Kellan when he'd made it clear that he was determined to stay out of her life?

She didn't owe Kellan anything. But she did owe Buck. Irina had no idea how long Kellan would be here in Royal, so if she was going to tell him at least some of the truth about his father, she couldn't wait for the perfect time.

"And," she muttered, slanting a look at the fire-engine red front door of the ranch house, "you're stalling."

Who could blame her, though? Being around Kellan was dangerous to the stability she'd been working on for seven years. She had a life now. She was no longer that frightened, shy woman just starting to be on her own. And she felt as if she was risking it all by being here. With him.

But that decision had already been made and putting it off now wasn't going to change anything. She reached for a brown leather briefcase on the passenger seat, took a breath and stepped out. A heartbeat later, though, the ranch house front door opened and a stunning woman with short, spiky black hair walked out. She was wearing a black coat, sky blue dress and mile-high heels, and she was laughing up at Kellan. He pulled his hat on while they talked, then the two of them crossed the wide porch and, at the top of the stairs, they stopped, hugged, then the still-smiling woman walked to her car, climbed in and took off.

Irina's heart felt…sluggish. Stupid. Of course there were other women in Kellan's life. Just because he had walked away from her didn't mean he had signed up to be a monk. It also didn't mean that she would enjoy seeing him with another woman. She hated that it could hurt so much.

Kellan turned his head, spotted her car and started down the steps. Irina couldn't put it off any longer, so she walked toward him. Now, after seeing the beautiful woman with him, she was gladder than ever that she'd taken the trouble to look good. Her long strawberry blond hair was loose, hanging in heavy waves down past her shoulders. She wore black slacks, a deep red long-sleeved shirt and a heavy black jacket. The wind whipped past her as if urging her to get back in the car and leave while she still could. From the corral, she heard a couple of cowboys shouting and the sharp, high whinnies of horses.

But all she could see was Kellan. He looked every inch the successful rancher. His dust-colored hat was pulled down low over his forehead, somehow highlighting the piercing blue of his eyes. The collar of his heavy leather jacket was pulled up against his neck. He wore a dark green plaid flannel shirt and jeans that hugged his muscular thighs and stacked on the toes of his scuffed cowboy boots.

Ironic that he was the epitome of the American cowboy that she had once dreamed about, as a young girl in Russia. But in those childish dreams, there had been love and a happy ending. Not a broken heart and the promise of more pain.

Irina took a breath, but she was afraid it wouldn't be enough to keep her calm. Every nerve ending in her body was awake and on alert. Her stomach did a slow swirl and her heartbeat thundered in her ears.

"Irina. I was coming to see you later today."

Then it was better she'd come to him. She didn't need him so close to her bedroom.

"Did I interrupt something?" she asked, nodding to where the woman's sleek black sports car was disappearing down the drive.

"That's Ellie Rae Simmons." He shook his head. "She's my executive assistant. Flew in from Nashville last night to take care of some business."

"Oh." His assistant. That should make her feel better, but that hug looked far friendlier than boss and employee. "It looked…different."

One eyebrow winged up as he tipped his head to one side to study her. "Jealous?"

She didn't even want to admit to herself that she'd felt a sharp pang of jealousy, seeing him with Ellie Rae. Kellan wasn't hers. Never had been. But seeing him with that woman had twisted her insides into tight knots that were only now beginning to loosen.

"Of course not," she lied smoothly. "I've no reason to be, do I?"

"No, you don't."

Well, that was honest anyway.

He folded his arms across his broad chest. "What are you doing here, Irina?"

"I want to talk to you about Buck."

Instantly, his features went coolly blank. "I don't need you to tell me about my father."

"I think you do." Of course, she couldn't tell him *everything*. She'd made a promise to Buck and she wouldn't break it. But there were things he needed to know.

"Irina," he said tightly, "let it go. Buck's dead and there's nothing you can tell me now that will change that."

"No. But there are things I can tell you that might change what you think of him."

He snorted.

She looked around. The cowboys were watching them now, curious. She recognized a few of them from seeing them around Royal, but now wasn't the time to say hello. Fixing her gaze back on him, she said, "Can we do this inside?"

It almost seemed as if he would refuse, but then he said, "Sure. Come on."

He stepped back to allow her to go first, and Irina felt his gaze lock on her. It gave her a chill that swiftly became heat. Apparently she had zero control over her body's reaction to the man. All she could do was hang on and hope her mind would win the battle.

"Let's go in here," he said, crossing the foyer into the great room.

She followed him and couldn't stop her gaze from

dropping to his behind, cupped so nicely by that worn denim. He set his hat, crown down, on a table, then shrugged out of his jacket and tossed it onto the nearest chair.

Irina took a moment to look around, since it was the first time she'd been inside. There was no hint of Christmas here, unlike at Blackwood Hollow. But the floor-to-ceiling windows on every wall offered amazing views of the ranch land and the yard and outbuildings. Sunlight flooded the space, highlighting the groups of overstuffed furniture covered in shades of blues and greens. The oak floor was gleaming and the wide expanse was broken up with dark red rugs. All in all, it was a comfortable room, with a distinctly male presence.

And, she thought, the words *distinctly male* described Kellan Blackwood perfectly.

Irina took off her coat and tossed it alongside Kellan's. She kept a tight grip on the briefcase she'd brought with her as she asked, "Why were you coming to see me today, Kellan?"

He shrugged. "I'm still looking for information, Irina. It's not a secret."

"Well," she said, "maybe I can help with that."

Surprise flashed briefly in his eyes. "I wasn't expecting that. Yesterday you were pretty clear about not helping me with Miranda."

"This isn't about your ex-stepmother," Irina said. "This is about Buck."

"No, thanks."

God, he was as stubborn as ever. His eyes were

cool, disinterested, and he might as well have been wearing a sign around his neck that read Not Listening.

"Kellan, he wasn't the man you think he was."

He laughed shortly, but there was no humor in it. "Is that right?" Shaking his head, he added, "Good luck convincing me of that. I knew the man my whole life, Irina. And you think you knew him better than I did?"

"Yes." She lifted her chin and fixed her gaze on his, so even though he was letting her see nothing he was feeling, he could at least see for himself that she was serious. "A father and his children don't always get to know each other as simply *people*. But I did know him like that and I can tell you that Buck helped people. A *lot* of people. Me included."

His gaze narrowed on her. "What're you talking about?"

Well, she'd come here to tell him the truth and she'd known that would mean sharing what he didn't know of her own story. But at least, he was listening. "You know I was married before."

"Yeah…"

She took a breath to steady herself before saying, "What you didn't know was that I was a mail-order bride."

"Are you serious?"

Surprise shone in his eyes again. Understandable. Most people didn't realize that sort of thing was still going on. But it was and she sincerely hoped that in most cases it turned out better for the "bride" than it had for her.

"My younger sister and I were orphaned when we were very young and we used to dream of coming to America." A small smile curved her mouth as she remembered, lying in the dark in the noisy orphanage, she and her sister whispering together. Making up dreams of love and husbands and being able to eat whatever and whenever they wanted.

"When we were older, Olga gave up those dreams and married a government official, but I joined an online dating service that matched up young Russian women with successful US businessmen."

"Why didn't you ever tell me?" His question interrupted her and she paused to answer.

"Because I don't like to think about it," she admitted, though the whole truth was that she hadn't wanted Kellan to know. It was embarrassing. She'd married a stranger in the hopes of a better life. And God, it was lowering for her to admit to having been duped.

Even as a model in Russia, her life hadn't been great. And when Olga's husband was transferred to a post far from Moscow, Irina had been desperately lonely. So when her friend suggested they both register on the mail-order bride website, Irina had taken a chance.

She swallowed her pride and continued, "Anyway, I was matched with Dawson Beckett, came to Texas and married him." She tightened her grip on the briefcase handle as if it were the one stabilizing point in her world. "Dawson was much older than me, and he had certain *expectations* of a wife that I didn't meet." She'd been young and so naive and so far from home or anyone she could go to for help. "He found ways to…convince me to meet them."

"He hurt you?" Fury in his voice warmed her heart even as Irina smiled but didn't answer. She wouldn't tell him what she'd suffered with Dawson. All the petty, demoralizing verbal abuse, along with the slaps, the hair pulling, the bruises in places no one else would see. There were some things she didn't want to relive, even in the telling of it.

"It doesn't matter now."

"Hell yes, it matters," Kellan ground out. "What the hell, Irina? Why did you stay with him?"

"Where was I to go?" she countered, defending herself, remembering her situation. "I didn't speak English well. I had no job skills beyond modeling. I had no friends to run to. I was in a trap that I'd walked into willingly."

He blew out a breath and shook his head. "You should've told me."

"By the time we met, it was over and I didn't want you to know," she said. "But my misery isn't part of the story. This is about Buck."

"How did my dad fit into this?"

She smiled. "I met your father at a dinner party. I was one of a number of foreign brides attending and Buck noticed how badly Dawson was treating me.

"One of my husband's friends was groping me and I slapped him. Dawson took me aside—" she took a breath before adding "—he hit me, in the ribs, where it wouldn't show." And in spite of the pain and humiliation of that moment, she smiled, remembering the rest of it. "Buck saw it all and he saved me."

The memory of Buckley Blackwood getting in Dawson's face and warning him to keep his hands to himself was still one of her favorites.

"Damn, Irina…"

She shook her head. "Anyway, Buck helped me get out of that marriage, gave me a job at the ranch and secured a work visa for me." She lifted her chin, met his gaze and said, "He offered to pay for my college and law school, but I would only allow that if he considered it a loan so I could pay him back."

She laughed a little at that, because in the end, Buck had won that argument, too. "In his will, Buck canceled my debt to him. My life has changed immeasurably, thanks to him. I came to this country looking for a prince to make my dreams come true. Now I am making my own dreams a reality. All because of Buck Blackwood."

"You're amazing."

"No. What Buck did was amazing," she insisted. "He helped me when he didn't even know me."

"I wish I could have seen Buck face down your ex," he admitted, and it sounded almost as if he was sorry it had been his father to ride to her rescue instead of him.

"It's not just me he helped," Irina continued quickly. "Buck paid off mortgages so people could keep their homes. He gave a young couple the money they needed to try IVF when they were desperate for a child. He sponsored children to summer camps.

He rebuilt an entire neighborhood after the last hurricane. And he did it all anonymously. I only know because he had me help him with much of it."

While she talked, she watched Kellan's eyes and was pleased to see that he was not only stunned but also a little humbled by his father's deeds.

"The only thing he ever asked," Irina added, "was that no one know who helped them. Of the few who did know his identity, as far as I know, I'm the first to break that promise to Buck. Because I think you need to know, more than Buck needs secrecy now."

"I don't even know what to say to all of this," he admitted and pushed one hand through his short hair.

Confusion shone in his eyes and Irina took a deep breath. She'd taken a chance in telling Kellan all of this. Especially about her own past. It wasn't something she liked to think about, let alone share.

Her brief abusive marriage was only a small part of her life, but it had been important in making her who she was now. In the years since then, Irina had learned to let the past go. To set that old pain aside and move on.

But she knew that was something Kellan had never been able to do. He'd lost his young wife in a car accident just a year before he and Irina had come together for that oh-so-memorable week. And she knew that pain would always be a part of him.

But he also used it as a club to keep away anything and anyone who might get too close to him, who might invite that kind of pain to revisit him. And as long as his past defined his present, his future would be empty.

Four

"You don't have to say anything, Kellan. But I wanted you to know that there was so much more to Buck than you were aware of."

Kellan felt shell-shocked. In a million years, he never would have pegged his father as some anonymous Santa Claus. Hell, he was surprised Buck had even *noticed* people in need, let alone helped them. Still, the fact that he had been kind to people outside their family didn't absolve him from doing a crappy job as a parent.

"I'm getting that," he said, nodding. "But as a father…"

"I'm not finished." Kellan watched her set the briefcase she'd been holding close on to the coffee table and open it up. There were four file folders inside. She grabbed the first one and held it out to him.

Wary, Kellan looked from the file up to Irina's eyes.

"You need to see these, too," she said and waved the file to encourage him to take it. When he did, he felt her watching him as he opened it, half expecting a snakebite.

"Buck had one of these on each of his children. None of you were talking to him, so he followed you all as best he could."

Kellan flipped through the articles, both newspaper and magazine, the pictures, the letters inside, and he felt the ground beneath his feet shift. There were things in that file he hadn't thought of in years. Big and small, all of his achievements, every piece of his life was all here. From his first newspaper interview to the day his real estate development company became the biggest in Tennessee. Buck had kept *everything*. Even Shea's obituary.

"He saved whatever he could find on you and your brothers and sister," Irina was saying. "He was a part of your lives in the only way he felt he could be."

A part of him softened toward his father. Had Kellan been wrong about Buck all those years? But as soon as he considered it, his mind argued, no. This file didn't excuse Buck's hard-ass attitude. His my-way-or-the-highway rule of life. His habit of cutting his own kids out of his life in favor of devoting every moment to his empire building.

Kellan's gaze snapped to hers. "He should have talked to us."

"Would you have listened?"

There was a ball of ice in the pit of his stomach and he didn't like it. He also didn't care much for that question because he knew the answer. "Maybe not."

She shook her head sadly. "Maybe he felt that it was too late to try to build bridges to all of you. Buck told me that he knew he'd lost all of you long ago. That he hadn't been there for any of his children. It was his one regret."

Again, he felt a twinge of…*something* for the father he'd never really known. Kellan couldn't stop flipping through the damn file. "But he didn't tell us that when he could have."

"No, he didn't. And maybe he should have tried," Irina admitted. "I tried to get him to contact all of you, but Buckley Blackwood was nothing if not stubborn."

"Yeah. I'll give you that much."

"He wanted to be a part of your lives," Irina said quietly. "He just didn't know how to get past the mistakes he'd made."

Kellan thought about that, and then a harsh laugh scraped his throat as he tossed the file back into the still-open briefcase. "Well, leaving our family home to Miranda sure wasn't the way to do it."

"I don't know why he did that," Irina said. "He never mentioned it to me."

"Nobody knows why Buck did anything," Kellan

muttered and scraped one hand across the back of his neck. There was too much new information storming in his mind. A new side of his father? What was he supposed to believe?

Irina was standing there, just one long step away, and she was watching him, waiting. It was killing him having Irina here. In his house. He'd steered clear of her for years because being near her was too damn hard. But now that they were here together, he couldn't imagine letting her leave, either. Maybe it was because she'd told him so much. About his father. About herself.

It drove him insane thinking about her all those years ago, alone and abused. If nothing else, he was grateful to Buck for stepping in to help Irina when she needed it most. But he couldn't figure out how he felt about the fact that Buck had been as involved in Kellan's life as he could be.

Thinking of the file his father had kept on him, he blurted, "He even saved an interview I gave to a tiny Nashville newspaper five years ago. Why the hell would he do that?"

Irina knew he wasn't asking her as much as he was throwing the question out to the universe, but she tried to answer anyway. "I told you. He loved his children. He just didn't know how to get past the mistakes he made."

Kellan lifted his gaze to hers and she saw pain and confusion in those sky blue eyes before he shuttered them to keep her from reading any more of his emotions. He and Buck were more alike, she thought, than either of them would have wanted to admit.

So she tried a different tack. "Buck helped so many people. Two of the stores on Main Street in Royal are only open now because Buck bought their buildings and sent the shopkeepers the deeds."

"What?"

She threw her hands up helplessly. "And a young couple trying to adopt? He paid all their fees and bought them airplane tickets so they could fly to China to get their baby."

He tossed the folder back into the open briefcase with the other three and scrubbed his hands over his face. "I can't decide if all of this information makes things better or worse for me. I didn't know the man you're telling me about, Irina. And bottom line? It doesn't change anything." Voice flat, he added, "Buck's still dead. He still left our family legacy to Miranda and shafted his own children. So all of this other stuff may only mean he was feeling old and trying to buy his way into heaven."

Impatience swamped her. "It can't change the past, true. But it could change how you feel about your father. Instead, you're determined to hate him, aren't you?"

"I don't hate him. Never did," Kellan argued. "But I won't pretend we had a great relationship. Or act as though his kindness to strangers makes up for the way he treated his own kids."

"No," she said, closing the briefcase and snapping

the locks. "I don't suppose you will. But I wanted you to know, because Buck deserved that recognition. He wouldn't claim it in life, but now that he's gone, I want you and Sophie and Vaughn to know what kind of man he really was."

He laughed shortly. "And don't you see the irony in that? You have to tell me stories about how he treated strangers to give me an idea about my own father?"

"Yes, I see it. But you don't want to see anything else."

"What else is there?"

She looked around the beautifully appointed but somehow *empty* room. This was Kellan. On paper, his life looked wonderful. Fulfilled. But in reality, he was a man alone and determined to stay that way.

Nothing could have been more irritating. "There's opening your eyes to the present and letting go of the past. I did it. I had to, to be able to have a good life." She wanted to tear at her own hair in frustration. "You are not the only one to have survived pain. But survival isn't enough, Kellan. You're letting bad memories cloud your vision so much that you can't see past them."

"This isn't about Buck, is it?" His voice was low, quiet. "None of this was. Not really."

Irina folded her arms across her chest and held on. She felt a little unsteady. Unsure. But it was too late to back down now. She'd wanted to show him a side of Buck he hadn't known, yes. But in doing so, she'd come up against a door to Kellan's past.

One he'd always kept locked and barred from her. And she'd hoped, ridiculously, that he would finally open it—and if not let her in, then at least step out himself.

"No," she admitted. "I suppose it's not."

"I'm not going to talk to you about Shea."

She flinched. Couldn't help it. "I wouldn't think so. You never would before."

One dark eyebrow winged up and his jaw went tight. "And how much did you tell me about your ex-husband? Nothing. That's how much. What did you say his name was?"

"Dawson Beckett," she snapped, and even saying the man's name left a bad taste in her mouth. "What should I have told you, Kellan? That I was foolish enough to marry a man I didn't know? That he was mean? Abusive?

"He used me to make himself look better. And Buck helped me get away. Your father intimidated Dawson into giving me a divorce. And I will always love Buckley Blackwood for that." She hated it, but tears gathered in her eyes. It always happened when she was angry, and right at that moment, she was furious. "I was young and stupid and wanted a new life. I got a nightmare."

Kellan took a step toward her and Irina backed up, holding one hand out to keep him at bay. If he touched her then, she'd crumble, and she didn't want to do that in front of him. Angrily, she swiped the tears off her cheeks and glared at him.

"Damn it," he said, clearly frustrated. "I didn't mean to hammer you with your own past."

She lifted her chin and tossed her hair back behind her shoulder. "Unlike you, I don't hide from my past, Kellan. I face it. I overcome it. I don't lock it away, because it made me who I am now. As much as I hate remembering my marriage, every time I do, it gives me strength to know that it didn't destroy me."

Kellan stared at her for a long moment and the tension building between them arced like a power line.

"And because I don't want to 'share' the most painful time of my life, I'm a coward? Is that it?"

"I didn't say that," she hedged.

He choked out a short laugh. "You didn't have to."

Irina took another deep breath. "Kellan, I know you lost your wife…"

"And my *child*," he ground out.

"What?" She swayed a little, not really sure what she was hearing.

He looked as though he wanted to bite his own tongue off for saying that out loud. But clearly, it was too late to call it back now. He scraped both hands across his face as if he were trying to wake up from a nightmare that had been haunting him for years. "Shea was pregnant. The *coroner* told me. I didn't tell anyone else."

"Oh God." She couldn't imagine what he'd been through, hearing about his lost child from a coroner. Not only had the woman he loved died, but she'd taken a piece of him with her.

Irina's heart ached. Literally ached. She'd had no idea and now she felt terrible for prodding at this wound. For forcing him to face a memory that had to tear at him. No wonder he was locked in the past.

As far as Kellan was concerned, he'd lost his future eight years ago.

"I'm so sorry." For his loss. For assuming she knew what he was dealing with.

He pushed one hand through his short, neat hair. "Don't. That's why no one knows," he said tightly. "I didn't want to hear 'I'm so sorry.' Or see the sympathy, the pity in people's eyes."

"I'm not offering pity," she countered. Though she really wanted to, she had known without being told that it wouldn't be welcome.

"Yeah?" His gaze locked on hers. "Then why do you look like you want to cry?"

"My God, Kellan." Completely exasperated, she continued, "I'm not a robot. I feel badly for you. For what you lost. That doesn't mean I'm offering you pity."

"Exactly what are you offering, then, Irina?"

Well, that was the question, wasn't it?

"I…" She took a breath, tried to settle her wild, racing thoughts and finally had to admit, "I don't know."

Kellan stepped up to her and she felt the heat of his body reaching out for her, wrapping itself around her. She nearly sighed but managed to stifle it. Irina knew she was in dangerous territory here, but she couldn't seem to care. Maybe it was because they'd talked more in the last fifteen minutes about the things that really mattered to them than they ever had before. And maybe, she thought, she was simply responding to the fire in his eyes.

"I think I know," Kellan whispered.

"I didn't come here for this," Irina said softly. She wanted him, of course. She always did. But today, she'd hoped only to reach him somehow.

"Yeah. I know that, too." His hands dropped onto her shoulders and Irina's eyes closed briefly at the rush of heat pouring through her.

This was not wise and she knew it. Worse, though, she didn't care. How could she? It had been seven years since she'd felt his hands, his mouth on her. She'd worked so hard to push thoughts of him out of her mind and yet here she stood, as eager for him as she had been the first time.

What was the definition of insanity? *Doing the same thing over and over and expecting different results.*

By that measure she was completely crazy.

"This is not a good idea," she said.

"Or," he countered, "it's the best idea we've had in seven years."

Amazed at that statement, she stared at him. "Really? You walked away all those years ago. Avoided me every time you've come back to Royal and now you think it's a great plan to slide back into bed as if nothing happened?"

He frowned and let his gaze move over her face like a caress before settling on her eyes again. "I won't apologize for leaving. It was the right thing to do."

"Maybe it was. For you." But she remembered how she had felt when he had left. As if he'd hollowed her out and left her an empty shell. Which she didn't want him to know. And that, she admitted, was pride. For a long time, she'd grieved the loss of him, wallowing in the pain because it was all she'd had left of him.

Eventually, though, she'd reassessed and realized that she didn't want a man who didn't want her. She'd asked herself, if Kellan had thought it was so easy to walk away from her, then why was she wasting tears on him? She'd worked hard to rebuild herself. To discover who she really was and what she wanted. Wouldn't going back now undo all of that work?

Or would it help to solidify her strength?

"Yes. And for you, too, as it turned out." His hands on her shoulders tightened a little. "You went to college. Now you're in law school…"

She frowned. "How did you know that?"

"You told me."

"I don't remember telling you."

"When you were busy defending Buck to me."

She frowned again.

"And now," Kellan said, "I hear you're an author, too."

"I *know* I didn't tell you that."

"Sophie did," he admitted. "What's the book about?"

"It's about starting over," she said. "When your world crashes down on you." That was the easiest explanation, and really, at the heart of it, that was her book.

"Maybe I should read it," he murmured, his gaze moving over her face like the lightest of touches.

"It's not finished."

"Fine. I'll buy a copy when it comes out."

"Why?"

"Does it matter?" He slid his hands to the column of her throat, then up to hold her face in his palms. "I missed you, Irina. Didn't want to. Tried not to. But I did."

"If that's supposed to be a way of flattering me, I don't understand it." His hands on her face, his thumbs stroking her cheeks, his eyes locked with hers.

"Understand this," he said and bent his head to hers. Irina held her breath as he took her mouth softly, almost tentatively at first. Then he deepened the kiss and Irina felt herself drowning. There was no air. There was no help. There was nothing but him. Just like seven years ago.

The moment that thought entered her mind, she pulled her head back and fought for the air he'd stolen from her. "I don't think I can do this again."

"It's just a kiss, Irina," he said tightly.

"It's more than that and you know it," she argued. Her body was humming and her mind was about to take a long vacation. Between them, a kiss was a lit match to dynamite. "And you don't have to look so pleased by that."

"Why wouldn't I?" His lips quirked. "Are you actually going to tell me you don't want to?"

"No," she said, because it would be pointless to lie. He could see the truth in her—just as easily as she saw the heat still glittering in his eyes. "I do want you. But doing this would solve nothing."

"Why does it have to?" he ground out. "Why can't it just be what it is?"

"Because..." She tried to come up with a reason, but she couldn't find one. Self-respect? Please. She had plenty of that and she wouldn't lose it by giving in to the need to be with him again. Pride? What did pride have to do with anything here? Really, why shouldn't they have sex? They'd always been good at it. Chemistry was never a problem for them. It was what came after that had always been their undoing.

"Not much of a reason," he taunted her.

She gave him a reluctant smile. "I'll find one. I only need a minute."

"Take two. It won't change anything." He moved in, closing the distance between them. "I want you. Always have," he admitted. "That didn't end when I left."

"But you still went."

"And will again," he agreed. His eyes were burning. His jaw was tight and his voice, when he spoke, was low and filled with an urgency that echoed inside her. "No secrets here, Irina. I can't stay."

"Won't."

"Either," Kellan said. "But this is now, Irina. We're here. Together. In this moment. So do we waste that? Or enjoy it?"

Was it that simple? Or was this a road studded with land mines that could blow up in her face and tear her heart to pieces again? Could she just "enjoy" time with Kellan and then let him go?

A tiny voice inside reminded her that she would watch him go anyway. Would it be better to stand strong and not know what it was to have his hands on her again—or would losing him be easier if she gave in to the fire sizzling inside and relished what they had while they had it?

Her breathing quickened and her heartbeat jumped into a gallop. She couldn't look away from his eyes. Maybe because she didn't want to. That settled it, as far as her body was concerned.

Missing Kellan had been like breathing for her. Inevitable. Unavoidable. Simply a part of her life. Irina had tried dating other men, but they had never quite measured up to the memory of Kellan. So instead, she'd buried herself in her studies, her job and, eventually, the book she was writing.

And somewhere along the way, Irina had convinced herself that she had a full life because to do otherwise was just too depressing.

But now he was here and she had a chance at— if not forever—then at least the opportunity to experience the magic of being with Kellan again. She'd be a fool to turn away. And she hadn't been a fool in a very long time.

Irina took a step toward him and his eyes flared in response. But he stayed where he was. He didn't reach for her. Didn't make a move. He was leaving this all up to her. He'd made his case, and now he waited to see what the answer would be.

Another man would push. Or try to sweet-talk her into his bed. But Kellan Blackwood was different. For him, it was all about people making their own choices. He was honest. Didn't make promises he wouldn't keep. Even seven years ago, he hadn't guaranteed her anything. So Irina had had only herself to blame for the misery she'd felt when he left.

Just as she would now.

Looking up into his eyes, she said, "We might regret this."

"We might," he agreed.

"And we're going to do it anyway."

He cocked his head to one side. "Are we?"

Irina gave him a half smile as she surrendered to the inevitable. "Was there any doubt?"

"Only from you," he said and finally, *finally*, reached out for her, his arms going around her with a strength that stole her breath.

She linked her arms around his neck, looked up into his eyes again—those amazingly deep, beautiful eyes—and said, "That's gone now."

"Thank God." He kissed her. Fiercely, desperately. His mouth took hers and his tongue claimed all that she was.

Irina's entire body lit up like the finale in Royal's annual July Fourth fireworks show. Her blood ran hot and fast, and an ache set up shop at the juncture of her thighs. This was what she'd missed. This was what she'd wanted from the moment she saw him again.

He tore his mouth from hers and then ran his lips and tongue along the column of her throat. She tipped her head to one side to give him better access. She shivered, in need, anticipation. How had she lived without this feeling? Without his touch? His kiss?

Her mind blanked out and her body took over. She lifted her right leg, hooked it around his hip and, when his hand cupped her butt to hold her there, she groaned.

"You've got too many clothes on," he managed to say.

"You, too." She ran her hands up and down his broad back, feeling his muscles shift and bunch. Irina wanted the feel of his skin against hers, the heat of the two of them, building, burning together.

"Upstairs." He threaded his fingers through her hair and dragged her head back, to look down at her.

Hunger was etched into his features. A need she shared seemed to be alive and pulsing in the room around them.

She cupped his face in her palms, kissed him, then whispered only "Yes."

Five

Kellan grabbed her hand and headed for the stairs. Thanks to her long legs, Irina matched his stride until they hit the first step, then they were running, taking those steps two at a time.

At the head of the stairs, Irina gave a quick look around. Pale gray walls, white oak floors and a dark green runner carpet going along the length of the hallway. There was a skylight overhead that allowed the watery sunlight to spill down onto them.

Then he was pulling her down that wide hallway to the room at the far end, overlooking the front of the house. He threw the door open and tugged her inside in one smooth move. Before she could catch her breath, Kellan slammed the door, then turned to grab hold of her. Irina went to him eagerly, her body practically vibrating with the tension he'd instilled in her.

All of the years between their last night together and this moment disappeared in a blink. Kellan's hands came down onto her breasts, and even through the fabric of her shirt and the bra beneath, she felt the burn of his touch. He tugged at the buttons, as impatient to touch her as she was to be touched.

A near-electric buzz erupted between them and Irina welcomed that oh-so-familiar feeling. It was as if they'd never been apart.

"Off," he said thickly. "Take that shirt off before I rip it off."

Another shiver because she knew he meant it and it thrilled her that he wanted her so much. She undid the buttons, pulled the red shirt off and tossed it aside. His first glance at her lacy black bra fired his eyes and dragged a guttural moan from his throat. "Man, it'd almost be worth it for you to keep that on—if I didn't want your nipples in my mouth."

"Since I want that, too…" She unhooked the bra and let it drop to the floor. His eyes went hot and fixed. Irina nearly groaned when he tore his own shirt off to expose his muscled, tanned chest. All she wanted now was to slide her palms across all that lovely flesh.

He must have been thinking the same thing, because the next couple of minutes passed in a breath of time and then they were naked, wrapped in each other's arms, tumbling onto his bed and rolling across the navy blue duvet.

The room was still and quiet. Outside, the sky was gray and a winter wind gusted, rattling the windowpanes.

"You're still so damn beautiful," he whispered, lowering his head to take one of her hardened nipples into his mouth.

"And you're still very talented," she whispered, arching her back, pushing herself into his mouth. His lips and tongue and teeth drew on her sensitive skin and sent her into a tightening spiral of escalating need. The duvet beneath her was cool but did nothing to dim the heat enveloping her. Irina scraped her nails along his spine and Kellan growled low against her chest. "You feel so damn good," he murmured as he shifted his attention to her other breast.

"Oh, so do you. And what you're doing... Don't stop."

"Not a chance," he vowed, voice low and guttural.

He swept one hand down her body, following the curve of her waist, the dip of her belly, to the center of her. Heat from his touch soaked through her skin, past her blood, down to her bones, and Irina felt as if she were burning up from the inside. *More*, she thought. She wanted *more*.

Then he slid two fingers into her depths, pressing, stroking. Her fingernails dug into his shoulders as she gasped for air. Irina planted her feet on the mattress, lifting her hips into his hand. It had been so long since she'd felt anything like this, her body was tight and ready to explode.

He suckled her and teased her core with steady strokes and caresses, and Irina knew she couldn't hold out much longer. She wanted him inside her when she climaxed, but she couldn't wait. Couldn't stop what was happening and wasn't entirely sure she would have if she could.

When that lovely, elusive feeling began to build at lightning speed, she braced herself for what was to come. Then her body came apart in his hands and all she could do was hold on. Blindly, she stared up at the beamed ceiling and shrieked when he pushed her over the edge into an orgasm that seemed to roll on and on.

Struggling for breath, body still trembling, Irina barely felt the surprise when Kellan shifted suddenly. He rolled over onto his back and pulled her with him until she was on top, staring down at him through passion-glazed eyes.

She smiled down at him, licked her lips and stroked her palms across his chest, her thumbs flicking at his flat nipples. He was gorgeous. The man's body was a work of art, all sculpted muscle and hard strength. Touching him filled her with the kind of desire she'd felt with no one else.

"Just a minute." He hissed in a breath and reached for the bedside table drawer. He yanked it open and fumbled for a condom, ripped at the packaging, then sheathed himself in only a few seconds.

"You should have let me put that on," she whispered.

He snorted. "If you had, it never would have gotten on in time. I'm teetering on a narrow ledge here, Irina. Won't take much to push me over."

"You say the nicest things." Irina gave him a small smile, then lifted both arms high over her head, lifting her hair and letting it slide down over her like a reddish-golden cape.

"And you're doing that on purpose." He reached out and cupped her breasts in his hands.

"You're a very smart man."

"Not at the moment," he said. "Blood supply's not going anywhere near my brain."

"I noticed." And her insides trembled as she stroked his chest again. She couldn't get enough of touching him, feeling all that coiled strength and banked heat beneath her hands.

She wanted him inside her. Deep. Hard. Fast. "How much more talking are we going to do?"

"I think we're done." He set his hands on her hips and lifted her up high enough that she felt the tip of him brushing at her core. Irina took a deep breath. Her gaze locked with his as she slowly, deliberately slid down his length, drawing him deep inside her.

With every inch of him she claimed, she felt that bone-deep stirring of need rise again. Along with a sense of "rightness" she hadn't felt in far too long. Watching his eyes, seeing the flames dancing there, fed the fire burning within her. When Irina rocked on him, he groaned her name and clenched his hands on her thighs. She felt the hard imprint of his fingertips digging into her skin, and she loved it.

Loved that he was so wild for her. Loved that he needed her. Loved that when they came together, nothing else mattered.

Irina threw her head back, braced her hands on his flat belly and rode him frantically. Every stroke pumped up the desire arcing between them. Every movement tantalized. Promised. Her hips set the rhythm that he followed. She listened to his breathing, fast, desperate. And she knew what he was feeling.

Irina took him deeper still, grinding her hips against his, creating a friction that drove them both faster, higher. How could she feel so much, so quickly after a shattering orgasm? How could she be so needy, so filled with the kind of desire that only Kellan could engender?

She looked down at him and etched his image onto her memory, so that she would always be able to draw up this moment in time and relive it. Far into the future, when she was living without him, when he was once again nothing more than a longing in the night, she would wrap herself in this moment and find the beauty and disregard the pain.

His expression was fierce. His eyes flashing. His jaw tight. He was…everything.

Gazes locked, Kellan reached down to where their bodies were joined and stroked that one spot that was filled with every beautiful sensation in the world. The moment he did, Irina's body and soul splintered again. A crashing wave of pleasure a thousand times stronger than the one before washed over her. Rocking her hips wildly, she called his name and rode that crest of satisfaction even as he claimed his own and emptied himself into her.

Then she collapsed onto his chest and felt his arms come around her.

Kellan cradled Irina to his chest and waited for his heartbeat to ease back down. Though the chances of that happening while he was holding a naked Irina seemed pretty damn slim. He'd known going in just how good sex with her was. But even he was amazed at what he'd just experienced. She had completely rattled him. His mind was a muddy blank and his body felt as if it had been wrung out and tossed aside.

If he had half a brain, he'd roll her off him and ease her onto the mattress. Regain a little distance between them. A safety zone. But not yet, he told himself, sliding his palms up and down her body.

She gave a soft, satisfied sigh, then lifted her head to meet his eyes. Her long strawberry blond hair was a tangle around her face and across her shoulders. Her dark green eyes looked like a forest at midnight—cool, impenetrable. And when her mouth curved slightly, his did, too.

"Damn if I haven't missed you," he said, reluctantly admitting the plain truth.

She shook her head and laughed a little and the

ripples of the sound slid into his heart. "No, you didn't miss me. You missed the sex."

"Well, yeah. It's pretty damn great." But she was wrong. He'd missed her, too. Missed the way she studied him as if looking for answers. Missed the way her hair smelled, like apples and summer. Missed that slight curve of her mouth and the way her eyes glittered when she climaxed. He missed her famous Russian Chocolate Salami and her ridiculous love of mint chocolate-chip ice cream.

Kellan felt a hard squeeze of his heart. Yes. He'd missed her. And that was a dangerous thing.

"You're right about that. The sex is wonderful." She rolled to one side of him and Kellan instantly wished she hadn't. In spite of knowing he should keep a buffer zone between them—for her sake, of course—he liked the heat of her, the sleek, soft slide of her body against his. Damn it. He might be in some trouble.

Scrambling to get under the duvet, she muttered, "It's cold in here."

"I can fix that." He reached for the bedside table, picked up a remote and clicked it.

Across the room, a gas fireplace leaped into life, with flames dancing across artificial logs. Outside, the wind was still whistling under the eaves and the gray sky looked darker now, more forbidding. And the ambient light in the room dimmed as if in sympathy.

"The fire's nice, thanks." She turned her head to

look at him. "I didn't get time for much of a look, but this is a nice house, Kellan."

He glanced around as if noticing for the first time. "Yeah, I suppose it is."

"But you do know it's Christmas, don't you?" she asked.

"What?" That came out of nowhere.

Leaning against a pillow propped against the heavy oak headboard, Irina held the duvet up over her breasts with one hand and waved her free arm to encompass the room. "Well, I really like this room—"

"Thanks," he mused, waiting for the *but*. It was a big room, with a massive four-poster bed, two leather club chairs in front of the used brick-and-stone hearth and an eighty-inch flat screen hanging above it. Right now, though, he'd have to say the bed was his favorite part of the space. "I'm pretty fond of it myself at the moment."

One corner of her mouth quirked. "I bet—but you need a Christmas tree in here. Right in front of the bay window. And at least one more downstairs in your great room. And lights. A lot of lights."

Kellan frowned as she talked. He knew that Irina was as much a fan of Christmas as his mother had been. As Shea had been. He really didn't celebrate Christmas. Hadn't since Shea died. What was the point? He was alone. He didn't need to be reminded of the holiday so that his solitude could be even more starkly defined.

But he wasn't going to get into that with her. Instead, he snorted and tried to make light of it all. "I don't think so. Just because the Hollow is lit up like a small city every December doesn't mean I carry that tradition on. That was all my mom's idea.

"Actually, it always surprised me that Buck kept that tradition going after he and Mom split up." Now that he thought about it, though, Kellan was pretty sure Buck had done it because it was expected of a wealthy man to put on a big show. And Buck had always done what was expected. Except for paying attention to his damn family, of course.

She turned her head to look at him. "That's a shame."

He shrugged, walked naked to the bathroom to clean up, then went back to the bed and got under the duvet himself. Without her warmth against him, he felt the chill in the room down to his bones. Not something he wanted to think about, or even acknowledge. Even to himself.

"Hardly a shame. I live in Nashville, remember? I'm almost never here," he said, hooking one arm behind his head.

"So you decorate at your house in Nashville?" Her tone said clearly she already knew the answer.

Kellan frowned. "No. Why would I? Just for myself? Pointless to decorate for Christmas when you live alone."

"That's a terrible attitude," she said, sliding her hands up and down the duvet covering her. "Christmas is a lovely time of year. It reminds us to take pleasure in small moments. To be thankful for what we have. That's never pointless."

Not for someone like her, he supposed. Kellan, though, didn't want to be reminded of heartbreak. Loneliness. Better to just close his eyes and try to get through December unscathed.

"Uh-huh." He glanced at her and attempted to change the subject. "Is this really what you want to talk about? Christmas trees?"

She shrugged. "Probably the safest possible subject."

"Meaning?"

Smoothing her hands over the duvet, she asked, "Would you rather start the sex-doesn't-change-anything-between-us conversation?"

Scowling, he went up on one elbow to look down at her. "Excuse me?"

"You know what I'm talking about," she countered, shaking her head as if shaming a two-year-old. "I can see in your eyes, that a part of you is already writing the speech. You're planning how to tell me that sex means nothing and that I shouldn't start building castles in the sky."

Irritated that he was, apparently, so easy to read, Kellan said, "I don't have to tell you that. You know it already. Right?"

"Oh, absolutely," Irina agreed, shaking her hair back from her face. Her green eyes fixed on him, she said, "I have no castles about you, Kellan. Not anymore."

No castles. He assumed that meant she wasn't indulging in daydreams about him. About *them*. That was good.

And even more irritating.

Seven years ago, he'd had to tell her that he was leaving Royal—and her—behind. She'd looked up at him like he'd just pulled the proverbial rug from beneath her feet. They'd shared an amazing week of sex and laughter and late-night feasts, naked in bed. But when their time was up, he'd left, determined not to make the mistake of getting too close with her again. He'd watched her eyes cloud with pain as he said goodbye. Heard a quaver in her voice as she realized that their time together was over.

What a difference seven years made. Clearly today Irina was the one in charge. He didn't like it.

"Let me save you the effort this time," she said, "so you can get rid of that worried scowl on your face."

Kellan deliberately eased his expression. "I'm not worried."

"Oh, I'm so glad." Irina's delicate, long-fingered hands still moved over the duvet as if she were stroking a beloved pet. "You don't have to worry about me, or about how I feel, because I won't be hurt again, Kellan."

"Didn't mean to hurt you then."

"And yet you managed." A small smile bloomed on her face, then disappeared again.

He hated hearing that, despite the fact that he'd known it even then. But there'd been no other way. Not for him. Royal had been choking him.

"I had to go. Had to get away from Royal." God, the memories of Shea had been everywhere. Kellan had felt as if he couldn't face the cowboys on the ranch or go into town without meeting a sympathetic face. He'd felt suffocated. Back then, it had been a choice to either leave town or die. And getting away from Irina had been imperative. Being with her had felt like a betrayal of Shea, so every time he looked at Irina, he'd felt that pain, too.

"You don't have to explain," she said, lifting one hand to stop him when he would have continued.

She tipped her head to one side and her hair fell in a strawberry blond curtain. "I survived. And now, I'm not the woman I was seven years ago. I've changed. Grown. And I can accept this for what it is."

Irritation mounted. Irrational? Maybe. But damned if he could stop the feeling. Still, he swallowed it back. "Okay, let's hear it. What do you think this is?"

"Just what you wanted back then," she said simply. "It's easy. No complications. It's two adults enjoying each other with no promises made or broken." Smiling, she sighed, then lifted both arms high and stretched languorously. The duvet dropped, baring her breasts to him, and Kellan wondered if she'd done it on purpose.

Reaching out, she cupped his cheek with one hand and said, "You're still frowning, Kellan, and there's no need. I promise you, I'm fine. We're good together. We're both still single. We're both dealing with the loss of Buck and so it's easy to come together—however briefly."

She looked so patient. So…sympathetic. Kellan wondered if that was how *he* looked when he was delivering this speech. Hell, he was being dismissed. Quite efficiently. Kellan was astonished and just a little dumbstruck. He'd said practically the same damn thing countless times. But this was the first time he'd been on the receiving end, and he had to say, he didn't like it.

Hell, was this what she'd felt all those years ago? Regret stabbed at him. Rubbing the back of his neck, he told himself to get over it. That he should be grateful for everything she'd just said. Instead, he felt like a gigolo being paid his fee and told to leave.

"You're looking worried again, Kellan." She laughed a little as she reached out to smooth his hair back from his forehead.

The touch of her fingers was light as air and yet penetrated right down into his bones.

"There's no need," she repeated. "I told you, I'm fine. My body feels wonderful and my heart is safe."

A fresh frown erupted on his face. He felt it and willed it away.

"So what now? We shake hands and part friends?"

"Oh," she said softly, "I don't think we'll ever be friends. There's too much past between us."

That bothered him, too, damn it.

"Psychoanalyzing us, are you?"

She laughed a little and turned her head until she was watching the flames in the hearth. "Oh, nothing so formal. Just acceptance of the reality of it all."

"I see." He didn't, but he would say it so he didn't

look like a complete idiot. Kellan much preferred being the one who laid down the rules in any romantic entanglement—not that this was romantic. Having Irina suddenly become the cool, calm, disinterested voice of reason was annoying.

The fan on the fireplace kicked into life and became a low hum as warm air drifted into the room, chasing the chill into the shadows.

"I know I said sex would be a mistake," Irina continued, and he had to lean in to hear her soft but firm voice. "But I don't think it was."

"Well, how fortunate for us." Sarcasm colored his tone and he wasn't sorry for it.

She ignored his jab and said, "I think it was a good thing for us to do this again."

"Happy to hear it." Sarcasm continued to drip from his words, but apparently, she didn't pick up on it. Or didn't care.

"Because now we know that we share chemistry—but nothing else."

Insult rose up now and tangled with the irritation but he couldn't find anything to say to combat her words. It wasn't just chemistry and they both knew it, in spite of what she said. That was the danger.

He'd always known it. Sensed that Irina was the one woman who could slip past his defenses and put him at risk again. Hell, that was the reason he'd avoided being near her all these years. It wasn't just chemistry. It was *more*.

"So I'm glad we did this." She nodded, as if encouraging herself. "I think it was good for me."

"Happy to help," he muttered. This was not going the way he'd imagined it. Kellan had known going in that sex with Irina was going to be world shifting. It always was. And he'd known that he'd have a hard time leaving her again.

What he hadn't expected was Irina having such an *easy* time of walking away.

"Kellan," she said and the faint music of her Russian accent flavored her speech, teasing him with memories of hushed whispers in the dark. "I almost want to thank you."

"Oh, sure." *Thank him?* He choked out a harsh laugh and nodded even while his insides were churning. "Why not? Be sure to leave a referral on the dresser before you go."

A ripple of laughter erupted from her and she reached over to give his hand a quick pat. "Why do you sound so insulted?"

"How should I sound?" He sat up, the duvet pooling in his lap, and looked down at her. Hand patting. Laughing. Hell, this whole episode had gone from X-rated to a damn farce. "Did you use me for sex to set yourself free?"

"Why?" she asked, still smiling. "Do you feel used?"

"Starting to," he admitted. Not to mention, more than a little annoyed.

She really laughed then and the sound rolled through the quiet room. He wanted to be angry but she was so beautiful when she laughed, he couldn't quite manage it.

When she caught her breath, she looked up at him and shook her head. "God, Kellan, now you sound outraged."

"Only because I am," he countered. Irritation was back, fiercer than ever, and frustration bubbled in the pit of his stomach. He was off balance. Unsteady, and he didn't like it.

"Damn it, Irina, what the hell's going on here?"

She touched his cheek briefly, then shrugged again, tugging the duvet up to cover her breasts. He couldn't have said why that gesture hit him so hard, but it did.

"The last time we were together, you walked away. And I had to watch you leave." Irina's dark green eyes locked on him. "You said you had to let me go for both our sakes. Well, this time, Kellan… I'm letting *you* go."

Six

Stunned speechless, Kellan stared at her for several long, tense beats. Before he could think of something to say to that, he heard footsteps pounding up the stairs at a dead run. He turned to face the door. Did he lock it?

His brother crashed in and stopped dead at the threshold.

No, he didn't lock it.

"Damn it, Vaughn! What're you doing?"

"Oops." Vaughn laughed, then nodded a greeting. "Hey, Irina. Good to see you."

She only smiled and said, "Hello, Vaughn."

Kellan glanced at her, astounded by her composure. No frantic tugging at the duvet. No embarrassment.

No reaction at all. Seven years ago, she'd been constantly worried they'd be found out. Today, she was stark naked beneath that duvet and she'd clearly just had sex with Kellan and she was as cool and serene as if she were at a tea party with the damn Queen of England. Who the hell *was* this woman?

And why was she even more intriguing now than she had been all those years ago?

Anger pulsing inside him, Kellan demanded of his brother, "Don't you knock?"

Vaughn lifted both hands and grinned. "Hey, middle of the afternoon. Who knew you'd be… busy up here?"

Kellan sighed. His own damn fault. *Should've locked the door.* "Go away."

One eyebrow lifted and Vaughn leaned one shoulder against the doorjamb, clearly going nowhere. "Is that any way to talk to a man who's bringing news?"

"Fine," Kellan ground out tightly. "What do you want? *Then* go away."

Obviously enjoying himself, Vaughn gave a one-shouldered shrug. "I was in town and heard something. Thought you'd want to know. Miranda's got her *Ex-Wives* show filming some scenes at the Hollow."

Kellan's head exploded. "Damn it!"

Lulu loved Blackwood Hollow.

The Bellamy, where the cast and crew were staying, was luxurious, as good as or better than any five-star hotel she'd ever stayed in and she had zero complaints. But this ranch house deserved at least ten stars, she thought.

The rooms were huge but cozy at the same time, and the grounds…from the tennis court to the swimming pools—two of them—to the hot and cold running cowboys all over… Well, she could see why Miranda had always described it so lovingly.

"It's an amazing place, isn't it?"

Lulu looked at Fee. They stood beside an enormous Christmas tree in the front window of what Miranda called the great room. Another point in the ranch house's favor—the Christmas decorations that filled the house. Lulu could only imagine how beautiful it all looked at night, with the lights glittering in the darkness.

"It really is," she said with a little sigh. "I could see myself living in Texas, if it could be like *this*."

Fee laughed. "I'd miss Manhattan, but I'd be willing to make the sacrifice." Staring out the window at the wide sweep of lawn and the seemingly endless Texas sky, now studded with dark clouds, she said, "You forget, don't you?"

"What?" Lulu studied her friend's wistful expression.

"That there's a whole world outside New York." Fee took a deep breath and let it slide from her lungs. "I mean, just look at the *space*. There's so much room here. You can see the entire sky. I'm more used to seeing patches of it with the high-rises crowding the image."

"True," Lulu said, turning her gaze back to the

ranch. "And really, the night sky is even prettier. So many stars."

Behind them, the crew was setting up for a shot and the other girls were enjoying the coffee and tea served by the ranch cook. Except for Miranda, who was upstairs looking for Irina Romanov.

"You had a good idea," Lulu said thoughtfully. "Having Irina as a guest star on the show."

Fee shrugged. "When Miranda told us about her, I talked to Nigel and he loved the idea. Said it would really get people talking. I mean who even knew mail-order brides even existed anymore?"

Lulu nodded, because she really didn't have anything to add to that. Nigel Townshend was the head of the studio and the producer of their show. He was smart and intuitive, so if he thought having Irina on the show would be a good idea, everyone else would go along.

Outside, the cowboys were working with horses in a corral painted a bright, shining white. An old dog pushed itself slowly to its feet and ambled up to one of the men, who absently stroked its head. It was such a different life from the one Lulu was used to; it was as if she were living in a documentary.

"Who," Fee murmured, "is *that*?"

Lulu followed her friend's gaze to the man just arriving in a big black truck. As they watched, he climbed out, slammed the door and tugged his hat on. He had sharp, handsome features, dark blond hair, and Lulu would have been willing to bet his eyes would be either blue or green. He was tall and muscular and walked with a slight limp that somehow only made him sexier.

"I don't know," Lulu said softly, "but he's pretty."

"Oh, he's more than pretty," Fee corrected.

"What are you two looking at?"

Lulu turned to smile at Miranda. "Just enjoying the scenery," she said. "That one in particular. Who is he? Do you know?"

Miranda took a look and nodded. "Sure. That's Clint Rockwell. He's got a neighboring ranch."

"Does he?" Fee murmured, tipping her head to one side to study the cowboy.

"He was a good friend of Buck's," Miranda said. "He used to help Buck out a lot, keeping an eye on things at the ranch. I guess he still is," she added as Clint walked over to the corral. "He's also a volunteer fireman for Royal."

He rested one boot on the bottom rail, then crossed his arms on the top one as he talked to one of the working men. Lulu was willing to bet that Fee was also noticing how Clint's jeans hugged his very nice butt.

"Cowboy *and* fireman?" Fee mused. "Interesting."

Lulu grinned. She hadn't seen Fee this interested in a man for a very long time. This could be fun. Then she turned to Miranda. "So where's Irina?"

"I don't know. She's not home, but her work is spread out across her bed, so she's probably just out on the property somewhere and will be back soon." Miranda touched Fee's arm. "Thanks for suggesting we have Irina on the show as a guest star. I think it will really help push her book."

Fee tore her gaze from Clint Rockwell long enough to smile at her friend. "It's no problem. I'm looking forward to meeting her."

Lulu hooked her arm through Miranda's and left Fee to enjoy the view. She herself wasn't interested in that cowboy, but she'd like more information about a certain lawyer. "Let's have some tea and cookies and you can tell me all about that lawyer friend of yours, Kace LeBlanc."

Kellan bolted, stark naked, out of bed and grabbed his clothes.

Instantly, Vaughn held both hands up and made a cross out of his fingers as if he were warding off a vampire. Turning his head to one side, he said, "Dude. I don't want to see that."

From Irina's perspective, she thought a naked Kellan was an excellent view. Of course, he wasn't naked for long.

"Kellan, what are you doing?" Irina watched him as he dragged on jeans, a shirt, and then sat down to put on socks and his boots.

"I'm going over to the Hollow to have a 'talk' with Miranda."

"Why bother?" Vaughn asked.

Kellan shot him a furious look. "If you don't care, why'd you rush over here to report it to me?"

Uncomfortable, Vaughn stuffed his hands into his pants pockets. "Thought you'd want to know is all."

Kellan scowled at him. "So you're okay with this ridiculous television show being filmed in *our* house?"

"Not my house," Vaughn argued stiffly. "Not for a long time."

"That's a damn lie. It's *Blackwood* Hollow. You're a Blackwood." Kellan stomped into his boots, then pulled his jeans legs down over the tops.

Irina listened to the brothers argue, but her gaze was locked solely on Kellan. He looked furious and she wanted to kick Vaughn for bringing the news. Not only had he gotten Kellan all worked up over Buck's will again, but he'd interrupted an important conversation. Irina was proud of herself for standing up for herself. For letting Kellan know that she wasn't the shy, timid woman he'd once known. But with the news of the film crew, she had a feeling everything she'd said had flown from his mind.

"It's Miranda's house, Kellan." Irina sat up a little straighter, clutching the duvet to her chest with one hand and pushing her hair back from her face with the other. She could see anger pulsing around him in thick waves, and she tried to calm him down. It didn't work.

"If you think I don't know that, you're wrong," he told her, slanting an angry look in her direction.

"Then what are you planning on doing?" She wished she could get up and go over to him, but she wasn't willing to stand up naked in front of Vaughn. And dragging the duvet with her would only make her trip.

"I'm going to remind her that this isn't over," he ground out. "I'm talking to my own damn lawyers and until this will business is settled, I don't want her putting the family ranch out on television for God and everyone to see." He stood up and glared down at her.

His eyes were frosty and she hated to see it. And still, she tried to talk him down. "It's just a TV show, Kellan. It's not that important."

His expression hardened and she knew that had been the wrong thing to say.

"Blackwood Hollow shouldn't be used as a backdrop to a bunch of silly women whose only claim to fame is being divorced from rich men."

Irina shook her head. "It's a silly show. Why are you so angry about it?"

He took a breath, scrubbed both hands across his face and finally answered, "Because I grew up in that house. Buck might have been a crappy father, but that house means something to me. I'm a Blackwood and so's he—" Kellan jerked a thumb at his brother "—whether he wants to admit it or not. Some things shouldn't be used like a damn sideshow, and my family home is one of those things."

She read that plain truth in his eyes and a part of her could understand it. But at the same time, Irina had to wonder if it wasn't more the pain of Buck overlooking his children in the will that was driving him right now.

"How're you going to stop it?" Vaughn asked and

Irina wished he'd go away. Unconsciously or not, he was feeding Kellan's anger.

Kellan swung around to face his brother. "I told you, I'm going to talk to Miranda. Set her straight."

"You're only going to make things worse, Kellan." Irina felt as if she were talking to a brick wall. But if she were, she could at least rap her head against it in frustration. "The fact is Buck left her the ranch. Legally, she can do whatever she wants there."

"You're in law school," he countered. "You know a will can be fought in court. Nothing's settled yet, so why take sides against me?"

She flinched at the jab, but she didn't stop. "I'm not taking her side. There are no sides, Kellan. And even if you are fighting the will, the fact is right now, the will says the ranch belongs to her. You can't change that."

Irina looked from Kellan to Vaughn and back again. Both Blackwood brothers were looking at her with accusatory glares. Apparently, Vaughn was no happier about this situation than Kellan was—he was just better at hiding his real feelings.

"I'm going to challenge that will, Irina, so don't bet on Miranda coming out on top." He walked closer to the bed and stared down at her with a coldness she hadn't seen since he'd walked away from her seven years before. "I'm damned if I'm letting that gold digger slither back here from New York and take what belongs to my family." He pushed one hand through his hair and muttered under his breath, "Buck must have been out of his mind."

"With that, I'll agree," Vaughn said and Irina sent him a look meant to shut him up. Instead, he gave her a smile and shrugged.

"You know the bottom line here, Irina?" Kellan asked. "I don't care about the money. Buck could have left her every single dime and I wouldn't have said a word. But our family home? The ranch? Blackwood bank?" He shook his head firmly. "No. Like hell am I going to sit still and take it." He started out of the room.

"Kellan," she called out, "wait for me. I'll go with you—"

But he was gone. Vaughn was still standing in the doorway, though, so she said tartly, "You set him off. You could at least go with him."

He shrugged. "No, thanks. Kellan wants to fight that woman, it's on him. I'm out."

"You're not fooling me, Vaughn." Irina watched him and saw his gaze shift from hers as if he couldn't bring himself to look her in the eyes "I know you're no happier than Kellan is with the situation."

His features went blank. "You're wrong about that. Anyway. Like I said, good to see you, Irina."

She tugged the duvet higher. "Uh-huh. Close the door on your way out."

Irina was only five minutes behind Kellan.

So when she raced into the house at Blackwood Hollow, the argument was still in full swing.

Miranda and Kellan were squared off in the foyer, in full view of everyone else, who were in the great room. She swallowed a groan when she saw that both cameramen were grinning as they kept their lenses focused on the arguing pair. Kellan had wanted to stop the filming. Instead, he was giving everyone quite a show.

"You've got no right," Kellan was arguing, his voice low and grim.

Irina heard the restrained fury in his voice and had to admire the way Miranda stood her ground against him. Actually, the woman looked completely relaxed, rather than cowed.

"Actually," Miranda said, folding her arms across her breasts, "I have every right. Do I have to remind you that Buck left the Hollow to me?"

He slapped his hat against his upper thigh. "No, you don't. But doesn't mean I'm not going to be right here, Miranda, fighting you every step of the way."

The other people in the room seemed fascinated by the confrontation. Irina saw amusement on the women's faces, and barely suppressed glee in the cameramen's expressions. And, Irina thought, Kellan probably hadn't noticed that the cameras were running. That everything he and Miranda were saying to each other was going to be preserved forever for the sake of the show.

Moving up to him quickly, she laid one hand on his forearm. "Kellan…"

He threw a quick glance at her and shook his head. "Irina. What're you doing here?"

She cast another look at their audience. "Trying to keep you from saying something you'll regret."

"Oh, don't worry," he assured her. "I won't regret any of this."

Miranda laughed a little and Irina sighed. Then she held on to his arm and tugged at him until he moved aside with her. Once she had his complete attention, she said, "The cameras are on, Kellan. They're recording you right now."

"What?" His head whipped around and he glared at the man whose camera was pointed at him. The other guy had shifted his focus to capture the women's reactions.

"Perfect," he muttered. Looking at Irina, he murmured, "Thanks for the heads-up. I didn't even notice. But they'll need a signed release from me to use any of it. And I'm not signing."

Before she could urge him to end this, though, he turned back to Miranda. Voice low, controlled, he said softly, "Miranda, I don't want you filming your silly show in my family home."

The other woman smoothed her hands down the front of her short black skirt. "It's my home now, Kellan. And the show isn't silly. It happens to have very high ratings."

He snorted. "From people with nothing better to do than watch you spend your ex-husbands' money?"

"You know," Fee pointed out from the other room, "there is more to us than that."

Kellan barely spared her a glance. "I don't care. I don't want it here. In my family home."

"I'm not arguing with you over this, Kellan," Mi-

"FAST FIVE" READER SURVEY

Your participation entitles you to:
✳ 4 Thank-You Gifts Worth Over $20!

Complete the survey in minutes.

Get 2 FREE Books

See inside for details.

Dear Reader,

Since you are a lover of our books, your opinions are important to us... and so is your time.

That's why we made sure your **"FAST FIVE" READER SURVEY** can be completed in just a few minutes. Your answers to the five questions will help us remain at the forefront of women's fiction.

And, as a thank-you for participating, we'd like to send you **4 FREE THANK-YOU GIFTS!**

Enjoy your gifts with our appreciation,

Pam Powers

To get your
4 FREE THANK-YOU GIFTS:

✳ Quickly complete the "Fast Five" Reader Survey
and return the insert.

"FAST FIVE" READER SURVEY

1	Do you sometimes read a book a second or third time?	○ Yes	○ No
2	Do you often choose reading over other forms of entertainment such as television?	○ Yes	○ No
3	When you were a child, did someone regularly read aloud to you?	○ Yes	○ No
4	Do you sometimes take a book with you when you travel outside the home?	○ Yes	○ No
5	In addition to books, do you regularly read newspapers and magazines?	○ Yes	○ No

YES! I have completed the above Reader Survey. Please send me my 4 FREE GIFTS (gifts worth over $20 retail). I understand that I am under no obligation to buy anything, as explained on the back of this card.

225/326 HDL GNQC

FIRST NAME	LAST NAME

ADDRESS

APT.#	CITY

STATE/PROV.	ZIP/POSTAL CODE

READER SERVICE—Here's how it works:

▲ If offer card is missing write to: Reader Service, P.O. Box 1341, Buffalo, NY 14240-8531 or visit www.ReaderService.com ▲

BUSINESS REPLY MAIL
FIRST-CLASS MAIL   PERMIT NO. 717   BUFFALO, NY

POSTAGE WILL BE PAID BY ADDRESSEE

READER SERVICE
PO BOX 1341
BUFFALO NY 14240-8571

NO POSTAGE
NECESSARY
IF MAILED
IN THE
UNITED STATES

randa said patiently but condescendingly, as if explaining something confusing to a three-year-old.

"Good." He waved one hand. "Then, until this is all settled in the courts, get these damn people out of our house."

"Kellan…" Irina kept her hand on his arm and gave him a little squeeze. "Just stop for now. This isn't the time."

"She's right," Miranda said, pitching her voice lower as her gaze met Kellan's. "You don't like the crew here? Well, you're giving them quite a show at the moment, Kellan. If you'll just leave, we'll be finished with the shot in no time."

"Finish now."

"No," Miranda said and Irina watched sparks fly in Kellan's eyes.

Irina grabbed his attention again. "Kellan, why don't you go talk to Clint? I saw him when I pulled up."

"Taking her side, are you?"

"No," she said. "But I'm not on yours, either. I just think neither of you will look particularly good on television if you don't stop."

His mouth worked as if he wanted to argue. His jaw was so tight it was a wonder the bones didn't snap. And his eyes were molten pools of fury. What did it say about Irina that she found him even more attractive than usual? Kellan was usually so controlled, so in charge, seeing him like this was exciting.

When her ex-husband had been furious, Irina had

made every effort to keep out of his way. But Kellan wasn't a violent man at all, so she'd never been afraid—or wary of him—as she had been of Dawson. Instead, she felt more drawn to him than ever. Did that mean she was stronger now?

Or was it just a measure of Kellan's innate appeal and sexual magnetism?

After what seemed like forever, Kellan said, "Fine." He kept his voice down and his gaze averted from the cameras. Then he shot one look at Miranda. "But this isn't over."

"I never for a moment thought it was," she whispered. Then, ignoring him completely, she turned to Irina and smiled.

Speaking more loudly, for the benefit of the cameras, Miranda said, "Irina, I'm so glad you're here. You're actually the reason we came to the house today."

"Me? Why?" Suddenly, she was the center of attention. Irina hadn't been expecting this. She looked at everyone in turn, then finally, back to Miranda, who was still smiling broadly.

"Because you're an amazing woman and I think the world should know it," she said with enthusiasm.

"Oh, for—" Kellan's muttered words broke off quickly when Miranda kept talking.

"When I was looking for you earlier," she said, "I found your manuscript pages on your bed. And since you did say I could read the first chapter, I did.

"Your book is wonderful, Irina. And I think it's

going to have a lot of meaning for thousands of women."

A flush of pleasure rose up in Irina. No one but her agent and editors had seen any of her work, so hearing Miranda rave about it meant more than the woman could have known.

"Come on now, you're a guest on our show and I want to tell the whole country about your book and when to watch for it!"

The whole country. Irina knew that the *Ex-Wives* show was popular, but she'd never really considered just *how* popular until right that moment. Millions of people would see her on this show. And though that thought was intimidating, she also realized that if even a small fraction of that audience bought her book, it would be amazing.

Dropping one arm around her shoulders, Miranda guided Irina into the great room, and introduced her to the women she hadn't met yet. Irina was suddenly relieved that she'd taken the time to dress well before going to see Kellan. And then she wondered if anyone looking at her would be able to see that just a half an hour ago, she'd been in Kellan's bed.

"This is Irina Romanov," Miranda said, showing her off as she would a prize puppy. "She works here at the ranch while she attends law school, and she's written a book that I'm sure will be a huge hit."

"Miranda…" She couldn't look away from the steady red light on the camera aimed at her. She felt like a rabbit being hunted. Or a deer caught in the headlights of an oncoming car.

Irina hadn't expected this opportunity and didn't know what to do with it now that it had happened. While she was both relieved and happy that Miranda had read and liked part of her book, she didn't know how to act in front of a television camera. When she was younger, she'd posed for pictures, but speaking on camera, meeting a roomful of strangers all at once was a little overwhelming.

She looked over her shoulder at Kellan and he was staring at her as if he'd never seen her before. No. It was more than that. The expression on his face spoke of betrayal. As if she'd somehow been in on Miranda's plan from the beginning. Like she'd arranged for this and somehow tricked him into making an ass of himself on television.

And the more she thought about that, the angrier she became. In spite of how close they'd been, it seemed he didn't know her at all.

His eyes bored into hers and Irina straightened her shoulders and lifted her chin in silent defiance. She wouldn't apologize for something she hadn't done. She wouldn't rush off to smooth the feathers of a man who was overreacting in the first place.

Those eyes of his were on fire and she could feel the heat despite the distance separating them. All around her, the women were chattering, throwing questions at her and Miranda gave her a nudge as if to wake her up. But Irina was wide awake already. She could be nothing else while staring into Kellan's eyes. Her body coiled and tightened inside, because it didn't matter what her brain was thinking, her body's reaction to the man was simply instinct.

When he slammed his hat down hard onto his head and stalked to the front door, she watched him go and a piece of her went with him. That, too, was outside her control. Seven years ago, it had nearly killed her to watch him walk away. Not this time. She wouldn't surrender her heart to a man who had made it plain that he wasn't interested in keeping it.

She had built a life without him and now it was time to take the next step.

"Why don't you tell us about the book, Irina?" Miranda was saying, and her tone said it wasn't the first time she'd made the request. Tugging Irina over to sit on the brown leather couch, she continued, explaining to her friends and most of America, "Irina was once a mail-order bride from Russia. She came here with nothing, isn't that right?"

Irina nodded, but didn't have a chance to speak because Miranda rolled right on.

"When her marriage ended, she reinvented herself and built a life." Miranda flashed her a bright, proud smile. "And I know that women everywhere will be inspired by her story."

Irina took a deep breath. Kellan was gone. She was on her own—just her and a few million people. That thought made her smile and Miranda beamed in approval. Lulu handed her a cup of tea and winked at her. Fee leaned in, grinned and asked, "So what was the mail-order husband like? And don't leave out any details."

Irina—overwhelmed, a little unsure of herself in the spotlight—laughed and took the next step.

Seven

It had been a long week.

Kellan hadn't seen Irina since that day at the Hollow when she'd joined Miranda and her traveling circus. The memory of Irina walking into the midst of those women and their cameras was still fresh and it still cut at him. Was she really so eager to sell her book that she was willing to work with the woman who had stolen his family's legacy?

He didn't have any answers and he hadn't had any damn peace since that day, either. When he managed to get a few hours of sleep, Irina was there. In his dreams. Naked. Moving with him—over him, under him—and then he'd wake up, frustrated and furious that she could have that much of an effect on him.

Kellan had met with Kace LeBlanc to talk about the will, and so far it looked like it wouldn't be an easy fight. But then, nothing about Buck Blackwood had ever been easy. The old man was dead and gone and still stomping on his kids.

"Earth to Kellan…"

Still simmering, he came up out of his thoughts and faced his little sister, sitting across the white-cloth-covered table from him. The Blackwood siblings were having dinner at the Texas Cattleman's Club and, since Vaughn was late, Kellan and Sophie were having a drink while they waited. It was early, so the dining room wasn't crowded, though a few of the old guard were comfortably seated at their usual tables.

The TCC had gone through a lot of changes in the last several years.

First and foremost, women were members now, too. A few of the old diehards had had plenty of issue with *that*. But the men who actually lived in the twenty-first century had applauded the change. The women had introduced other changes to the club that had been long overdue.

Now there was a day care center, and the interior of the club was brighter and less like a man cave, thanks to a much-needed paint job and an extensive remodel. The old building now had much bigger windows and higher ceilings, giving the whole place a feeling of openness it had really needed.

"Yeah, sorry, Sophie."

He caught one of the waiters checking his little

sister out and Kellan sent him a scowl that had the man scuttling away for the safety of the kitchen. Hard to admit that his little sister was a beauty. Also hard to ignore since everywhere they went, men were constantly admiring her. Tonight, she wore a dark red dress that was a little too short for Kellan's comfort and dipped a little too low over her breasts. Her long auburn hair was pulled back from her face to fall in a thick wave down her back, and her brown eyes were sparkling.

A sign that he hadn't spent enough time in Royal over the years. When he first moved away, Sophie was only twenty years old. In the time he'd lived away from Royal, she'd become a beautiful woman and Kellan felt as if he'd missed more than he'd ever wanted to. Vaughn had changed, too. He'd become more insular, more separate from Royal and the family. Had he taken a cue from Kellan? He didn't like the thought of that.

"I don't even want to know who you're scowling about," she said, then stopped. "No. Wait. I *do* want to know. Irina?"

"No." He fired a hard glare at her. He was specifically avoiding thinking of Irina. When he could. "Where'd that come from?"

She shrugged. "Vaughn told me he caught you two in bed, so I figured you guys were together again."

"Vaughn's got a big mouth," he muttered, then added, "We were never 'together.'"

"Not how I remember it," she said, picking up

her dirty martini, "but whatever helps you sleep at night." She took a sip of her drink, then set the glass down again. "Anyway, like I was saying before you zoned out, thinking about Irina—"

"I wasn't—"

She ignored that and rushed on, "For all my big plans of snooping around town to get dirt on Miranda? I haven't been able to find out anything." Disgusted, she toyed with the stem of her drink glass and admitted, "I've asked everyone I can think of. Heck, just hanging out at the diner, I can usually overhear plenty of gossip, but the only thing people are talking about is the television show and how exciting it is because someone they know—Miranda— is on it.

"And the other women on the show? I kind of like them, especially since they have no problem gossiping about anything under the sun... But they don't know anything about Buck's will or why he left everything to Miranda." She sighed dramatically. "Apparently, if there is a secret, she hasn't shared it with her friends."

"It's only been a week, Soph," he said, sipping at his scotch. Though he had to admit that his sister should have picked up on *something* in that time.

"I know. It's just frustrating." She tapped her dark red nails against the table. "Gossip is usually much easier to come by in Royal. And gossip about the television show does me zero good."

But did it? Irina leaped into his mind again. He couldn't help remembering how she had sailed into the ranch house and right onto the TV show like it had all been scripted. Had it? Was she somehow in cahoots with Miranda in all of this?

Why the hell else would she have been so cavalier about sex? That wasn't the Irina he knew. She was definitely the hearth-and-home type—but now she was suddenly live and let live? No. Something else was going on.

Maybe she'd been working with Miranda right from the beginning. He suddenly remembered those files of his father's that she'd shown him. Well, she'd shown him only his own file, but he'd spotted three others in that briefcase. She'd said that Buck had kept a file on each of his children... But there had been *four* files, not three. So what the hell was that about?

"Are you even listening to me?" Sophie demanded.

"What? Sure. Of course."

She rolled her eyes. "Nice recovery. So what's going through your head that isn't me and my complaints?"

He wasn't about to dump all of what he was thinking onto his little sister, so he said only, "Miranda. It always comes down to Miranda. She and that film crew are all over town." And now they had *him* on camera and he knew damn well they would use the footage.

He'd talked to a lawyer about the fact that he hadn't signed a release. Apparently, that would have been enough to force them to cut Kellan from the show if he'd pressed the point. But he'd reconsidered at the last minute. Sure, he wouldn't come off looking great, but neither would Miranda. And it suited him to have the whole damn country knowing exactly what he thought of his gold-digging ex-stepmother.

"Yeah, I know. Vaughn and I talked about it. He pretends he doesn't care about Blackwood Hollow, but he does," Sophie said, taking another sip of her drink.

"Maybe." Kellan shook his head as if to dislodge the dozens of random thoughts scuttling through his mind. It didn't help. His eyes were gritty and there was a constant tightness in his chest. Facing Irina again after all this time had been harder than he'd thought it would be—not to mention dealing with all this other stuff. "Anyway. Like I said, it's only been a week. It'll probably take even *you* longer than that."

"Thanks. I think." Sophie's fingers trailed up and down the stem of her glass. "But I was thinking…"

"Never a good thing."

"Funny." She nodded to him. "What do poor, lonely women do when they don't have brothers to irritate them? Anyway, if I can't discover anything here, I think I'll go to New York. Talk to Miranda's friends. Maybe go to the studio, see what I can find out."

Frowning thoughtfully, he said, "They're not going to let you into the studio. Or tell you anything once you're there."

"Please." She waved that off. "People always talk to me. Especially men."

He held up one hand. "I don't want to hear that."

She grinned. "Anyway, I think New York is where we might get some answers."

"Fine. But give it another week or so. Poke around some more in Royal, see what you get."

She sighed. Sophie had always been the impatient one. She wanted things done and done *now*. But in this, she'd have to slow down, Kellan thought. All of them had to agree to a plan before they made a decision.

"All right. A week."

"Maybe wait until after Christmas," he said suddenly.

"I'm sorry. Did you just say you're going to be here through Christmas?" she asked.

He hadn't planned on it, but now… He couldn't see going back to Nashville before he got this mess settled. And he was already here, so why not? "Yeah. Probably."

"A Christmas miracle!" She clapped her hands and gave him a grin. "The Blackwood siblings together at Christmas? Who would have thought that could happen again?"

A twinge of guilt pinged inside him as he realized that in cutting the holiday and Royal out of his life, he'd done the same to his siblings. Why had he never considered that before? He was fighting so hard for the ranch, the family legacy, but he wasn't paying close enough attention to his *actual* family? Made no sense.

Still, seeing the gleam of excitement in Sophie's eyes had him backtracking a little.

"Don't make more of it than it is," he warned.

He wasn't even sure why he was doing this—staying in Royal through Christmas. Since Shea died, he hadn't celebrated the holiday—had, in fact, avoided even thinking about it. But now things felt... different, somehow. Was it Irina? Was it fighting for his family's legacy? Hell, was it as simple as actually spending time with Vaughn and Sophie again? He didn't know. All he was sure of was that he wasn't ready to leave. To go back to his empty house in Nashville.

"Oh God, no," Sophie said, laughing. "This is enough for now."

"Agreed."

"What're we agreeing on?" Vaughn pulled out a chair and sat down. Then he lifted one hand in a signal to the waitress. "Let me guess. Is it that we hate Miranda? Or is this about Kellan and Irina hooking up?"

"What are you talking about?" Kellan demanded.

"You know exactly what he's talking about," Sophie said with a sad shake of her head. "So spill. You and Irina. Together again?"

"No." His gaze narrowed on her.

"They looked pretty together to me," Vaughn mused, then said thanks to the waiter who delivered his usual, a longneck beer.

Sophie smiled and picked up her drink, lifting it in a toast. "Vaughn says Irina looked very cozy in your bed."

He swiveled his head to glare at his brother. "You had to shoot your mouth off?"

"Didn't have to," Vaughn corrected. "Wanted to." He grinned and took a swig of his beer.

"You're not a monk, Kellan," Sophie reminded him. "You and Irina are both adults. Irina's great, so why are you so touchy about it? Tell me everything."

"Nothing to tell."

"Oh, that's sad." She shook her head slowly in mock sympathy. "A naked woman in your bed and nothing to tell? Well, you are getting older…"

Vaughn snorted.

"Not what I meant." Kellan downed the rest of his scotch and signaled the waiter for another. He was already rethinking the plan to spend more time with his siblings. "I meant, it's none of your business. Either of you."

"If it was," Vaughn pointed out, "it wouldn't be as much fun."

"True," Sophie added.

"Enough."

His sister held one hand up for peace and shot a warning look at Vaughn. "Okay, we'll stop."

"Good."

"I'll just say—"

He sighed.

Sophie rolled right on. "—that I like Irina. And it would be good to see you happy again, Kellan."

"I am happy."

"Yeah," Vaughn mused sarcastically. "You're a blazing ball of sunshine. Nearly blinding just to be around you."

"Why're you here?"

"You invited me." He shrugged.

"You're not happy," his sister argued. "At best, you've been content, Kellan. That's different from happy. You haven't really been happy since Shea."

Where was that waiter? "Not going there."

Even Vaughn looked surprised that Sophie had brought up Kellan's late wife. But she wouldn't be stopped.

"It's been eight years, Kellan," she said softly. "You lost Shea and we lost *you*."

He winced at the well-aimed jab.

"I know how much you loved her," Sophie added. "We all did. But maybe it's time to let her go."

His sister's words echoed in his mind, his heart. Memories of Shea weren't as clear as they had once been. Even the pain had been muted over time, though he knew that a part of him would always grieve her and the loss of what they had had. But, Kellan admitted silently, even if it was time to let Shea go, he wasn't sure he knew how.

Two days later, the whole town was buzzing.

The "teaser" trailer for Irina's upcoming episode on *Secret Lives of NYC Ex-Wives* had gone viral and now it was all anyone in town was talking about.

Irina simply had *not* been prepared for the reaction to the video.

"Irina! Hi!"

She turned to wave at a blonde high-school girl working for Jillian at Miss Mac's Pie Shack. "Hi, Trina."

"Really looking forward to your show." The girl grinned. "You must be totally excited!"

"Thanks, I am," she said and silently added, *I think*. She kept walking down the crowded sidewalk, smiling and nodding at those she passed. How did celebrities handle this all the time? People watching you. Wanting to talk to you. She gave another wave to the town barber and then the florist, and still, Irina walked, headed to the diner.

It was Christmas-shopping time in Royal. The streetlamps were twined with garlands and winking white lights. Banners hung across the street wishing people Have a Royal Christmas in swirling golden letters. And the sidewalks teemed with busy shoppers. Parking was impossible on Main Street since it was packed with cars, so she'd been forced to park at the other end of town. And this long walk was proving, beyond a doubt, the power of the internet.

She'd lived in Royal for more than seven years, and yet this was the most notice anyone had ever taken of her. She'd never had the time to make real friends. When her marriage ended, Irina had withdrawn into herself, needing time to rediscover herself. Remember who she had been before Dawson Beckett entered her life.

Then between working at the Hollow, going to night school and finally law school and writing her book, Irina's life had been fairly insular.

Until today.

Irina felt exposed in a way she never had before. People she'd never spoken to had seen that viral video. Had seen Miranda and the others talking to her about her marriage. Her book. They knew about her divorce. That she'd been abused. It was mortifying and she had no idea why she hadn't considered the consequences before she'd agreed to appear on that show. Still, the whole story would be out when her book was released, so maybe it was good to get used to this now. Maybe.

But it wasn't only *her* people were speculating about. Everyone was talking about Kellan's confrontation with Miranda, too. She'd long heard that there was nothing the town of Royal liked better than juicy gossip. And thanks to that video, she was seeing the proof.

She wondered what Kellan thought of all this. But she was wondering about him a lot lately. Like, what he was doing? Was he thinking of her at all? Did he miss her even a tenth as much as she missed him? She'd tried to deny it to herself, but the plain truth was she ached to be with him.

"Irina," someone else called out, splintering her thoughts, "that show sure looks like it's going to be fun!"

She smiled at the hairdresser and kept going. What was she supposed to say to people she barely knew?

"Can't wait to read your book," someone else said in passing.

Her smile never wavered as she walked. Her book. That was what she should concentrate on. Surely this publicity had to be good for potential book sales. So she would suffer through being stopped every few feet and keep in mind that she was helping herself in the long run. Irina plastered a smile on her face and determined to find the silver lining.

Until someone came up behind her, slid one arm around her waist and said, "Hello, darlin', it's been a while."

Irina stiffened instantly. She would never forget that voice. How could she? She still heard it in her nightmares. Instinctively, she tried to shift out of his grasp, but Dawson Beckett only tightened his hold and gave her a hard, bruising pinch at her waist. "Don't. Just keep walking. Everyone will think we're old friends. We'll talk a minute and then I'm gone."

"Go now," she said, nodding at a woman who passed her on the sidewalk.

"I don't take orders from you, bitch." He kept a tight grip on her, holding her pressed against him. "I saw your video."

She closed her eyes briefly. In all the rush of the book and the TV show, Irina had completely forgotten that with the teaser going viral, Dawson would be sure to see it. It was clear that he was furious, too. And in spite of how far she'd come, she felt a ribbon of fear slide through her.

"Let me go, Dawson," she muttered, drawing on courage she had lacked completely when she was under this man's thumb. Yes, there was fear, but she wouldn't surrender to it. "Or I will scream so loudly, Sheriff Battle will hear me."

"Oh, you shouldn't do that." Dawson smiled down at her and it was feral. He hadn't changed, except to get more gray at his temples. He was about five foot ten and was still barrel-chested, with small dark eyes and a grand handlebar mustache he waxed and turned up at the ends.

Another hard pinch. "And you best watch how you talk to me."

Wincing from the pain blossoming in her side, she ground out, "What do you want, Dawson?"

Another hard pinch. Tears burned her eyes but she blinked them back. She wouldn't cry in front of him. Never again. He liked it too much.

"Well, that's the question, isn't it?" He stared off down the sidewalk. "What do I want?" He paused as if thinking about it. "I don't like being talked about, Irina. People who know you were my wife are doing some whispering and that's not good for my business."

Irina took a deep breath to steady herself.

"And that book of yours," he added, "is already causing me some grief and it's not even out yet. I've got people looking at me different…"

"No more than you deserve."

"You should know better than to make me mad, Irina." Another vicious pinch and he gave her a tight smile. "I figure you owe me, girl. Without me, you'd have had nothing to write about after all."

Stunned, she stared at him. "Really, you would take credit for what you did to me?"

His voice dropped to a dangerous note she had hoped to never hear again. "There you go, making me angry again. Don't you remember what happened when you didn't do what you were told? You know it doesn't work out well for you."

A chill swept along her spine because she did remember. All too well. She'd lived with Dawson for two years of hell, and had thought that she was doomed to be there forever. But he was out of her life now. She was free of him. She'd fought hard, with Buck's support, and she'd carved out a new reality for herself. Damned if she'd be dragged back into Dawson's web. She didn't answer to him anymore.

He grimly steered her through the crowd and Irina caught more than a few people looking at her in curiosity. Could they see pain on her face?

"The book isn't about you, Dawson. It's about overcoming misery and building a new life for myself."

"You calling me a misery?"

"Among other things," she said tartly and refused to be afraid of him. All he could do was briefly cause her pain. He couldn't rule her life any longer.

They were almost at the diner, and the crowd of people outside seemed to give him pause. He drew her to a stop, turned her to look into his eyes and said, "I had a deal go bad on me today thanks to that video. Cost me ten thousand. You owe me that money."

"I owe you nothing," she said and began to get angry at herself for allowing him to hurt her. She didn't have to do what he said. Didn't have to fear him, either. That Irina was gone.

"Not a good idea to treat me this way, darlin'," he murmured.

"I'm not afraid of you anymore, Dawson."

"Well, you better rethink that, because if you don't get me that money, I can find ways to make you miserable, little girl."

He probably could. Though he wasn't as rich as Buck Blackwood, he had money. And worse, he knew influential people with as few morals as he had.

"You're blackmailing me?"

"Well, you don't have big-shot Buckley Blackwood standing guard over you now, do you?"

No, she didn't. It shamed her to admit that she missed having Buck to rely on. Briefly, she thought about reaching out to Kellan, but it had been a week since she'd seen him and the way they'd left it, she couldn't imagine him standing up for her. So she'd have to do it for herself. "I don't have ten thousand to give you."

"You will once that book of yours comes out."

"That's not how publishing works." She'd gotten a small advance and wouldn't get the other half until she turned the completed book in. As for royalties, she hoped she would get some eventually, but there was no guarantee. So if Dawson wanted money from her right away, he would be disappointed. And a disappointed Dawson, as she knew, could be dangerous.

"I don't give a good damn how it works. You find that money or—"

"Or what, Dawson?" Disgusted with this ghost from her past and her own response to him, Irina finally pulled away from his grasp. She just managed to not rub the spot on her side that he'd pinched so hard.

"Or I'll remind you with more than a pinch."

She hated that even though she was different now, he could still make her afraid. Hated that her old response was still the first thing that occurred to her. "I'll go to the police."

His eyes went hard and cold. "Wouldn't advise that, darlin'. I've got a lot of important friends in Dallas. They'll sit your small-town sheriff down and tell him how things'll be."

She met his gaze. "You don't have friends, Dawson. You have people you use."

His eyes narrowed. "Gotten mouthy, haven't you? Just remember. Accidents happen all the damn time. Pays to be careful."

"Irina!" Lulu called her name from outside the diner and waved one hand to get her to hurry up.

Thank God. Irina took a deep breath and looked at Dawson. "I have to go."

"That's fine." He took a step back. "I'll be around."

He would, too. She knew this wasn't over. Walking away from him now was just a small reprieve. Dawson wouldn't go away until he had what he wanted. And even then, there was no guarantee he wouldn't come back. Irina walked on and didn't look back. She didn't have to. She could feel Dawson's dark eyes boring into her back.

But she smiled for Lulu and happily listened to the woman laughing and chatting as they went into the diner. Ordinarily, Irina would have enjoyed spending time with her and Miranda and Fee. She didn't know the other girls as well, but these three women had become important to her over the last week or so.

They were her first real friends since leaving Russia. When she was married to Dawson, he'd kept her on a tight leash. She hadn't had a lot of opportunity since to establish friendships. And over the last week, she'd realized how much she had missed having another woman to talk to. Insularity was good, but apparently, she still needed people, too.

"Who was that old guy you were with?" Lulu tugged her over to a booth where the others were gathered.

"He's just…an acquaintance of Buck's." She didn't want to talk about Dawson. Didn't want anyone to see the remnants of fear still clinging to her.

They accepted that, these new friends, and she was grateful. She was also grateful for the noise, the laughter and the tableful of food and drinks. The film crew had decided to have a "wrap" party of sorts at the diner. Of course, they'd still be filming for a while, but they'd finished what they'd wanted to accomplish at Blackwood Hollow, and as Fee had said, "Any excuse for a party!"

Irina picked up a glass of iced tea and sipped at it while she listened to everyone. Glancing around the crowded diner, she smiled to herself. The locals were loving it, really enjoying watching these reality television stars in their own hometown. Everyone seemed relaxed, happy...except Kellan.

How had she missed him when she'd walked in?

She caught his eye from across the room. He was seated at one of the red vinyl booths and across the table from him sat his "assistant," Ellie Rae Simmons. Naturally, the woman looked beautiful, dressed in a navy blue long-sleeved dress and black heels. She was smiling at Kellan, apparently not noticing that *he* was looking at Irina.

The power of his gaze locking onto hers was nearly a physical jolt. A week since she'd seen him and he hadn't been out of her thoughts longer than a few minutes at a stretch. She'd missed him. Missed his touch. Missed his scowl. Missed the way his mouth moved when he was trying not to smile.

Kellan's gaze fired and Irina's body responded with a flush of heat that swamped her. Didn't matter that she was in a room full of people. It was as if she and Kellan were completely alone. All that mattered was the arc of electricity buzzing between them. Every cell in her body was shouting at her to do something about this now that he was there. *Right* there.

But she didn't want to see him now. Couldn't deal with him and what she was feeling. That buzz of attraction to Kellan was tangling up with the irritation and fear she'd felt at seeing Dawson again. Her body was still jumpy and she felt in desperate need of a shower to wash away her ex-husband's touch. Nope. She couldn't do it. Couldn't stay at the party—not with Kellan there.

She told herself that no one would miss her. The crowd had gotten thicker in just the last few minutes, with the locals and the Exes, as Fee called them, laughing together like old friends. So Irina set her glass down on the lunch counter and left, forcing herself to avoid Kellan's gaze.

The wind was cold and snatched at the hem of her coat, blowing her hair into a tangle. She put her head down, determined to avoid speaking to anyone. She wasn't worried about Dawson approaching her again. He'd said what he had to say and he wasn't a man to repeat himself—as she had reason to know.

Besides, after the viral video, Dawson wouldn't hang around town because he wouldn't want to run into people he knew. Dawson's tentacles reached all over Texas. She could almost understand that— now that she'd talked about her failed marriage, it wasn't only excitement she'd seen around Royal that morning. Irina had also seen the same kind of interested, curious, sympathetic glances Kellan had complained about. Now she knew what it felt like, having people discuss her life. To have them watching her with kind, but curious, eyes. And she felt a whole new sympathy for him.

"Which," she told herself, "he wouldn't want at all."

"Talking to yourself?"

Eight

Irina jolted. For the second time that day, a man had come up behind her. She really needed to pay more attention to her surroundings.

"Sorry," Kellan said. "Didn't mean to scare you."

She took a breath and blew it out. "Well, you did." She kept walking, ignoring the ache in her side that Dawson had left with her as a reminder, until Kellan took her arm and drew her to a stop.

"What's going on with you? Why'd you leave the diner?"

"It's nothing, Kellan. I'm just not in the mood for a party."

"Yeah," he studied her. "Looks like more."

"Well, it's not." Now he had to get insightful? She

pulled her arm free, nodded at the woman hurrying past them with several shopping bags. "Shouldn't you be with your 'assistant'?"

"Meeting's over."

"Looked like a friendly one," she said and immediately wished she hadn't. She sounded jealous. Maybe she was. How pitiful was that? He'd already made it clear, both in the past and only last week, that there would be nothing more than sex between them. And hadn't she taken a stand, as well? Told him she was letting him go? That she wasn't going to have her dreams crushed again?

But she *hadn't* let him go. That had been pure bravado and she hadn't been able to back it up, damn it.

"I didn't come after you to talk about Ellie Rae."

Irina stopped on the sidewalk, dragged windblown hair out of her eyes and stared up at him. "Then why did you?"

An older man stepped out of the hardware store and grinned. "Kellan. Boy, my granddaughter showed me that clip of you going after Miranda. Want you to know I'm going to be watching the whole show."

Kellan grimaced. "Great. Thanks, Bill." When the man walked on, Kellan muttered, "My own fault for signing the release just so the country could see what a fortune hunter Miranda really was. Now I can't go anywhere without someone talking about that stupid show."

"Then maybe you should stay home." Maybe she should have, too.

"Why the hell would I hide?"

"I don't know." She shook her head. Tired. She was suddenly so tired. "And I don't care, either. Goodbye, Kellan." *Just walk, Irina. Just walk and get somewhere quiet. Somewhere safe. Where you can think.*

He tugged her to a stop again.

Once more, she pulled free. The difference between him and Dawson was that Kellan didn't hold her against her will. At the moment, though, Irina felt pushed beyond what she could deal with and she just needed to be alone. "I'm not in the mood for this, Kellan."

"That's why I followed you." He looked into her eyes and she wondered how much he was seeing. How much he could sense. She tried to take the fear, the worry, out of her gaze, but that was impossible. All she could hope was that he either wouldn't notice or wouldn't say anything.

"You're shaken."

"It's cold," she said defensively.

"I didn't say *shaking*," he countered and gave a quick glance at the heavy Christmas-shopping traffic on Main Street. "Come on," he said, taking her hand and pulling her along beside him.

"Stop it, Kellan. I'm going home."

"Right again," he said. "*My* home."

"No." She stopped dead. If he wanted her to go with him, he would have to literally drag her behind him. Her emotions were too wild, too uncontrolled right now. Too close to the surface. She couldn't trust herself with him. Couldn't be sure she wouldn't blurt out something stupid. Something she wouldn't be able to take back.

"Damn it, Irina," he said and idly lifted one hand to greet someone behind her. "Something's wrong. I can see it."

His blue eyes shone with concern, and at any other time, she'd have been happy to see it. But she was too needy now and if she gave in to the urge to lean, even just a little, on him, she would end up dumping everything on him. She didn't want to do that. "If there is, it's none of your business."

"Maybe not," he admitted. "And I can see why you would believe that. But…if you think I'm going to back off when you're clearly in trouble, you're crazy."

A huge part of her wanted to accept what he was offering. Yet at the same time, she didn't want to draw him into the mess that was Dawson Beckett. "You can't do anything."

"Try me."

His eyes met hers. She stared up into those deep blue eyes and saw determination, tangled with worry, and Irina sighed. Kellan wasn't going to give up on this. Though he had walls built around his heart, he was also the kind of man who would badger her until she told him what was wrong. Even if that meant they stood on that crowded sidewalk all day.

"Fine," she said, surrendering to the inevitable. "I'll go to your house. But I'm taking my own car because I'm not staying for long." When he nodded, she turned to walk away and stopped when he spoke again.

"I'll wait for you. You can follow me home."

She tipped her head to one side to look at him. "Worried I won't show up?"

"No," he said coolly. "Worried you're too upset to be driving. So I'm going to make sure you get there in one piece."

Instantly, Irina knew he was remembering that his late wife had died in a traffic accident and she regretted being so snotty. God, talking to Kellan sometimes felt as if she were tiptoeing through a minefield.

Nodding, she said, "Fine. I'll follow you."

In fact, seven years ago, she would have followed him anywhere. Then he broke her heart. How humiliating was it to admit, even to herself, that nothing much had changed?

"Is Vaughn here?"

Kellan watched her wander the great room, unable to sit. Unwilling to let her guard down. She kept moving as if she could avoid talking if only she was busy enough. Her arms were folded across her chest and her teeth continually chewed at her bottom lip.

He'd known the minute he spotted her in the diner that something was very wrong. Irina's features were so expressive and her eyes so open to the world that she was easy to read if you knew what to look for. Kellan didn't like seeing her this way. It bothered the hell out of him that she was this agitated and still keeping the reason for it from him.

And it was shocking as hell to him to silently admit that seeing her upset tore at him until he felt as if he couldn't breathe.

"No," he said, finally answering her question. "Vaughn went back to Dallas for a couple of days to take care of some business."

Kellan hadn't expected to miss his brother's presence. Hell, this was the longest they'd been together in years, and yet having him around had been... good. He'd enjoyed being able to spend time with his baby sister, too. In fact, he'd actually enjoyed simply being back in Royal, and he hadn't expected that, either.

Kellan had spent years avoiding his hometown, his family, *anything* that would remind him of his loss. Of Shea. Now being here, that old pain was somehow lessened. For some reason, he'd thought that Royal would remain unchanged, as if it was in a bubble, and coming back here he would be assailed with memories so thick he wouldn't be able to see clearly.

Instead, the town had moved on, his family had, too, and it was only Kellan clinging to the past. Coming back, he'd rediscovered a sense of belonging, while at the same time he'd learned that his memories of Shea were softening, until they looked in his mind like a Monet painting—misty, shrouded in wisps of remembrance that hid the pain and left the happiness. He didn't know what to think about that, so he put it away and focused on the woman who haunted his every thought.

Even knowing something was bothering her didn't take away from the bone-deep attraction he felt for her. In her dark blue jeans, forest green tunic-style sweater and black boots, she looked…amazing. Her strawberry blond hair tumbled down her back in a tangle of curls and waves, tempting him to thread his fingers through that silky mass. But drawing on his willpower, he buried his need and focused on her.

"Tell me what's going on."

She whipped her head around to look at him. "Is that an order?"

"Where's that coming from? When have I ever *ordered* you to do anything?"

She waved one hand and admitted, "You never have. I know that."

"It's a request. Talk to me, Irina."

"Why?" She stared at him. "Why is this important to you, Kellan?"

He couldn't explain that. Not to her. Not to himself. He only knew that having her trust him enough to talk to him was more vital than anything ever had been before. Maybe he didn't have the right to her trust. Maybe he'd given that right up seven years ago. But he was here now. And that had to count for something, didn't it? "Because maybe I can help."

She shook her head. "Why would you want to? There's nothing between us, Kellan. You've made sure of that."

Yes he had. Seven years ago. But only a week

ago, it had been Irina calling a halt to whatever it was that burned between them. "You're the one who pulled away this time, Irina."

"Before you could do it—which I'm sure you were about to do."

"We'll never know now, will we?" Though inside, he had to acknowledge that she was probably right. "It doesn't matter, anyway. Tell me what's wrong."

She pushed both hands through her hair, turned around to face him from across the room until she was backlit in front of the window. Outside, the wind was blowing and the pines growing in the yard bent and dipped in the strength of it.

"Fine," she said, releasing a pent-up breath. "My ex-husband found me on Main Street. He's—" she laughed harshly "—unhappy about the show. About my book. He wants money and I don't have it to give him."

"He's blackmailing you?" A surge of anger charged through Kellan with a strength he wouldn't have believed possible.

"*Extortion* would be the technical term." She folded her arms across her chest again and whipped around to stare out the front window, avoiding his eyes. "Are you happy now?"

"Happy?" He stalked across the room in a few long strides. Grabbing her shoulders, he turned her to face him. "Hell no, I'm not happy. I'm pissed. That he came at you. That you were alone. That I had to browbeat you to get you to tell me."

She pulled away from him. "Don't. Don't grab me, Kellan."

He let her go instantly. He didn't like the slight tinge of panic he'd heard in her voice. "I'm sorry."

Sighing, she said, "No. I'm the one who's sorry. It isn't about you, Kellan. It's Dawson. He always grabs hold of me—like I'm a rag doll or something."

"I'm not him." And it pissed him off that she would compare him to her dick of an ex even for an instant. He could understand it, but that didn't make it any less annoying. He'd never hurt a woman in his life and loathed the men who did.

"I know that." She laughed again and it still sounded pained. "God, I know that, Kellan." Taking a deep breath, she looked up at him and whispered, "This was a mistake. I shouldn't have come here."

"Why not?"

"Because I need some time to think."

"Bullshit."

"What?" She blinked at him.

"You heard me." Kellan laid both hands on her shoulders—gently, carefully—to make sure she knew that his touch was nothing like her ex's. Thankfully, she didn't flinch or try to get away. "You don't need to think about this, Irina. You already know what you have to do. You need to talk to Sheriff Battle. Nathan will know how to handle this guy."

She laughed harshly and the sound was like breaking glass. "I told Dawson I would and he said he would have important people step in and make sure the sheriff couldn't help me."

"And you believe him?" Kellan shook his head and kept his gaze locked on hers. "Come on, Irina. The man's a bastard. He specializes in hurting you. Making you afraid. Why would you take his word for anything?"

She stared into his eyes for what felt like forever, before she slowly nodded. "You're right." Pushing her hair back from her face, she took a deep breath. "I should have realized that on my own—" She held up one hand. "And I probably would have once I'd had some time to myself to think it through."

"Yeah, you would have," he said with assurance. "I just helped you see it sooner is all."

Frowning a little, she asked, "Do you really believe that?"

"Of course I do," he said and wanted her to believe it, too. She'd picked herself up after a disastrous marriage and built a wonderful, successful future for herself. Kellan admired the hell out of that. "You're a smart woman, Irina. You'd have figured out that the bastard was just trying to keep you from going to the police for help."

She huffed out a breath. "God, he was, wasn't he?"

"Yeah." Kellan nodded and gave her a half smile. "But you're stronger than he thinks you are. You survived him. You built a life. His coming after you like that tells me that *he's* the one who's afraid."

One corner of her mouth turned up at the thought. "You think so?"

"Count on it. Now. You're going to see Sheriff Battle, right?"

Her head cocked, she looked up at him. "I am. That's what I have to do."

"I'll go with you." And he wouldn't take no for an answer on that point. He was going to stand beside her until Dawson Beckett was sent back to whatever rat hole he'd climbed out of.

She nodded again. "Yes. Thank you. I'd appreciate that."

"Okay, then." Glad that was settled and that he didn't have to push her to accept his help, Kellan pulled her in for a hug, wrapping his arms around her and holding her tight.

"Ow!" She pulled away and he had to admit he really hated when she did that.

But not nearly as much as he hated the flash of pain in her eyes. "What's wrong?"

She rubbed her side and shook her head. "It's nothing."

"Irina..." While she avoided his gaze and brushed off his concern, Kellan focused on where she was rubbing. Fury rose up within him like waves crashing against the base of a cliff. "He hurt you." It wasn't a question.

"It's nothing."

He kept his voice even, though his blood was pumping thick and hot. "Show me."

Her mouth worked as if she would argue, and

then finally, she walked away from the wide front window. She kept walking until she was in the empty foyer, standing beneath a skylight through which watery sunlight drifted into the room.

"Vaughn's not here, you said. Is anyone else?"

"No," he ground out, looking down at her. "It's just us."

Nodding, she slowly pulled up the hem of her sweater.

Kellan spotted the angry reddened skin at her ribs and knew that by tomorrow, she'd be black-and-blue. He fought for control. Fought to contain the rage that raced through him. His hands fisted at his sides and everything in him wished he had that bastard in front of him. He'd make the man pay for putting a mark on her skin and fear in her eyes.

"Dawson prefers pinching to punching," she said, already dropping her sweater.

"Don't," Kellan urged and caught the hem of the heavy knit fabric. Lifting it again, he smoothed his fingertips gently over her burgeoning bruise and saw her eyes mist over. From pain? Humiliation? Anger? He couldn't be sure, though she had the right to feel all three and more.

Slowly, he went down on one knee in front of her. "Kellan…"

"Shh." He leaned in and kissed her bruise. Gently, carefully, his mouth, his lips covered every inch of the mark Dawson Beckett had left on her as if he were trying to wipe the man out of her memory.

She sighed and swayed toward him, and that soft

sound fed a different kind of fire inside Kellan. His hands slid up her legs and cupped her behind while he continued to kiss her bruised skin.

"That feels good," she murmured.

"So will this." He tipped his head back, smiled at her and then let his hands find the waistband of her jeans. With her gaze locked on him, he quickly undid the snap and zipper and then dragged the denim down. Kellan saw the flash of passion dazzling her eyes and was grateful that every trace of fear was gone now.

"You have great legs," he whispered. "Always did like them."

He glanced at the lacy pale pink panties she wore, then hooked a finger in the waistband and pulled them down, as well.

"Um, Kellan. What're you doing?"

"I think that's pretty clear," he said with a wink.

"I thought you wanted me to go to the sheriff…"

He smiled. "Later. Unless, you want me to stop."

She pushed her fingers through his hair and pulled his head closer to her. "No. Absolutely not."

Desire flashed hot and fast inside him, and Kellan immediately fed that need. "Lean against the wall."

"Now, that's an order," she said, "but I'll take it."

He grinned and eased her legs apart, before covering her with his mouth. She gasped and then tugged his hair, pulling him tighter to her body. His tongue swept out, tasting, teasing. She shuddered in his grasp, but she held on, demanding more.

He gave it to her. He slid one hand from her butt

to the inner depths of her heat while his mouth worked that tiny bud of sensation. Again and again, he licked her, suckled her, while his fingers claimed her from the inside. He couldn't get enough of her. The tiny sighs and sounds slipping from her throat electrified him. His skin was buzzing. His blood, pumping. His heartbeat thundered in his ears.

Kellan couldn't feed the need inside him fast enough. Touching her. Tasting her. He wanted her more than he ever had. Needed her more than he would have thought possible. She was strength and vulnerability and confidence and anxiety all at once, and that incredible mix drove him crazy with desire. With a want that never left him.

And now he knew she'd been hurt.

Someone had threatened her and he hadn't been there to help. Someone had abused her and Kellan hadn't been there to stop it. Regret, fury, pain whipped through him, twisted with the desire still churning inside him and fueled the need to touch, to claim.

"Kellan—I can't—" Her breath was wild now, her speech broken in short bursts. Her body trembled but she opened her legs even wider, instinctively wanting more of what he was giving her.

He delivered. His tongue flicked madly against that sensitive bud until he felt her shudder, heard her muffled shriek as her body splintered under his attentions.

While her breath was shattered, her pulse racing, he stood, drawing her jeans and panties up as he did. Then he swept her into his arms, lifting her off her feet.

"Or," she said breathlessly, "we could wait until my knees stop shaking and I could walk on my own."

He didn't want to wait. Didn't think he *could*. Kellan dropped a fast kiss on her upturned mouth and said, "Let me feel manly."

Her laughter spilled out around him and Kellan was glad to hear the real pleasure in it. At the top of the stairs, he paused, looked down into her eyes, held her close and felt something shift inside him. Something fundamental. Something…elemental. And while the world around him swung out of its usual orbit, Irina lifted one hand and cupped his cheek.

He turned his face into her touch and kissed her palm. "You dazzle me."

A half smile curved her mouth and completely did him in.

Then she stilled, her forest green eyes shining with secrets she wasn't saying. And maybe that was all right for now. Because in this moment, they didn't need words.

Irina cupped his cheek in the palm of her hand and Kellan turned his face into her touch. Silken heat filled him along with another, more nebulous feeling he didn't want to identify. Didn't want to think about. Yet he remained *dazzled*.

"Show me," she whispered.

There was nothing he wanted to do more. Kellan carried her to his bedroom and inside. He closed and locked the door—just in case—then set her on her feet. Like a dance, she moved into his arms, lifted her face for his kiss, and when their lips met, Kellan felt the spark of it right down to his bones.

The kiss was gentle, passion muted, but there, simmering between them as they gave and took and shared breath by breath, Kellan fell into the spell of her.

Slowly, they undressed each other, hands skimming over flesh, exploring, caressing. She tipped her head to one side and he kissed the curve of her neck, inhaling her scent. He could have spent hours like this, simply reveling in the feel of her soft skin beneath his hands. Still, cupping her breasts, feeling the soft sigh of her breath, made him want more. Feeling her hands moving over his back, his chest, and then down to his already aching erection, made him need.

He saw her eyes blaze with heat and knew that her desire, like his, had climbed to a fever pitch. When he walked her back toward his bed, she smiled up at him as he eased her down onto the bed. She smiled again and undid him. His gaze locked onto hers. "Feels like it's been forever since I was with you."

"It always feels that way for me," she admitted.

"I missed you, Irina." A part of him couldn't believe he was admitting the truth to her after all this time, but he didn't stop. "And it wasn't just the sex. For seven years, I missed *you*."

"I missed you, too, Kellan. So much."

His right hand skimmed over the marks that

Dawson had left on her and he felt another jolt of helpless fury. "I hate that he put his hands on you."

"I don't want to think about him now. I never want to think about him again, but especially not now. Besides," she added as she stroked one hand across his chest, "you already kissed it and made it better. Remember?"

His mouth tipped up in a small, knowing smile. "Well, then, I'll focus on the rest of you now. How's that?"

"A wonderful idea." She reached for him, but he shook his head and stepped back. If he didn't get suited up right away, he'd lose all control and forget to stop. He dipped into the drawer of the bedside table for a condom and quickly put it on. Then he stretched out on the bed alongside her and focused entirely on Irina.

It was as if he were seeing her—really seeing her—for the first time. The gray half-light in the room seemed only to illuminate her. She shone. Everything about her was breathtaking.

Her hair spilled out on either side of her head, her deep green eyes were fixed on him. Her mouth, that amazing, wonderful mouth, was curved in a knowing smile, as if she could sense what he was thinking, feeling. And if she could, she knew what would happen next.

Kellan dipped his head to claim one of her nipples and he felt the sharp jolt of desire as it whipped through her body. He was attuned to her, too. He knew what she liked, and he did everything he could to push her beyond her limits. To take her to the very edge of sanity and then to join her there.

He ran his hands up and down her body, while her hands curled into his shoulders, her short, neat nails digging into his skin. Abandoning her breast, his mouth took hers in a deep kiss that demanded as much as it gave. Their tongues tangled together and their strained, desperate breathing was the only sound in the room.

He slid one hand down to the nest of strawberry blond curls at the juncture of her thighs and then beyond, into the heat. Into the tight, wet core of her. She came off the mattress, rocking her hips into his touch. He lifted his head, stared down into her passion-glazed eyes and watched her frantically try to find the release his fingers were promising her.

"Kellan," she managed to say around a gasp for air, "be inside me. Let me feel you fill me."

Now it was his turn to feel that desperation, Kellan admitted silently. With those words, she'd pushed him beyond the limits of his patience.

"Yes. I need that, too." And he did. More than his next breath.

Kellan shifted position and in one long, slow thrust, claimed her body and gave his to her. She took his face in her hands, pulled him down for a kiss. Her long, beautiful legs came up and hooked around his hips, pulling him deeper and higher inside her. He rode her hard, then gently, changing the rhythm up to keep them both off their guard. To chase the climax and then let it go before it could end everything.

Kellan never wanted it to end. If he could stop time, he'd do it now, he thought, with his body buried inside hers. Kellan's heart raced. His eyes locked with hers and he saw the first glimmer of satisfaction hit her and watched it build as she brokenly cried out his name. She held on to him, as if he were the only safe place in the world, and he felt the same. This moment. This incredible, moving moment was all that mattered.

His hips pistoned, because the climax was more important than the journey now. She held him, shuddering, shaking, and finally, he took that wild jump, following her into that bright oblivion.

Minutes later, Kellan's heart was still pounding and he was still reeling from the power of that orgasm. He felt her hands smoothing up and down his back and knew that no matter what, he would always be able to draw up the memory of those butterfly caresses against his skin.

He looked into her eyes, their bodies still joined, locked together, and he felt his world take another hard jolt. Kellan didn't want to think about what it might mean, but he couldn't deny it was happening. Slowly, silently, he rolled onto his back and drew her with him, until Irina was lying on him, her head on his chest, her legs tangled with his.

And if he could have found a way to manage it, he'd have stayed like that forever.

Nine

"Do you want to press charges?"

Two hours after leaving Kellan's bed, the two of them were in the sheriff's office in Royal. She'd told Nathan Battle everything and he hadn't said a word through the whole thing. He'd simply listened intently, letting her know he was taking in every word. Now he looked her square in the eye and waited for her answer.

Irina took a deep breath, glanced at Kellan, then back to Sheriff Battle. "No."

"Are you sure about that?" Kellan asked, his voice quiet.

Half turning in her chair, she looked at the man she'd been so intimate with just a couple of hours ago. His eyes were fixed on her with heat and under-standing and…an emotion she couldn't read. But she knew that something had changed between them. Something monumental. Irina had stopped hiding from the truth.

She was in love with him. Still. Always. She could tell herself she was going to walk away. Heck, she'd told *him* that she was letting him go. But the truth was she would love him until the day she died. It was as simple—and as sad—as that.

Because she had to accept that Kellan wasn't look-ing for love. Would never be able to move past the memories of his late wife to build a different future than the one he'd once seen. Whatever love he had to give, he'd already given to Shea. There was no room for anyone else in his heart. Irina couldn't pre-tend otherwise.

But she also couldn't deny her own feelings. Couldn't deny herself the opportunity to be with the one man who touched her heart and soul and body.

"Yes," she finally said, wanting Kellan to under-stand. "I'm sure. I don't want anything else to do with him, Kellan. I don't want court dates where I'll have to see him. I don't want him to be a part of my life at all anymore. If he leaves me alone, I'll do the same for him."

He looked as if he wanted to argue the point, but she was relieved when he didn't. Irina was sure that if he had his way, Dawson would be charged, arrested and slapped into jail. But for her, it was enough to beat him. To let him know she wouldn't be cowed or threatened or afraid. To show him that she would stand up for herself. Once he understood that, Dawson would move on to an easier victim. She knew that much about him.

Still holding her gaze, he nodded slowly.

"All right, then." Kellan looked at the sheriff. "What do you think, Nathan?"

Nathan Battle shrugged and leaned back in his chair. He ran one hand through his short, brown hair and turned his gaze on Irina. "I think the decision is yours, Irina. Whether or not I agree with it isn't important. Either way, I'll be having a talk with Beckett. I'll make sure he knows we frown on hurting women. And that blackmail's not going to fly around here, either."

Irina closed her eyes briefly. She'd already shown Nathan the bruise Dawson had given her and she'd seen the same fury in his dark brown eyes that she'd seen in Kellan's gaze. Strong men, she thought, were especially furious at a man who abused others.

"Thank you," she said.

"No need to thank me," he said. "It's my job. And my pleasure to take care of this for you. Don't you worry about Dawson Beckett. He might think he has friends who can shut me down, but he's wrong.

"The man's well-known to law enforcement in this part of Texas," Nathan added, tapping a pencil against his desktop. "He straddles the fence between crook and entrepreneur and usually manages to keep his balance. But he's been known to slip from time to time."

"I feel like even more of a fool now," Irina said. She'd believed Dawson when he said that the sheriff could do nothing against him. But he wasn't a businessman; he was a criminal and the law knew it.

"Well, you shouldn't. Beckett's the one who was a fool." Nathan smiled at her. "He should have recognized a strong woman when he saw her."

She took a breath and smiled. "Thank you."

"Yeah, thanks, Nate," Kellan put in, and then, as if to lighten the mood in the small, ruthlessly organized office, he asked, "How's that new baby of yours?"

Nathan's face lit up. "She's great, but not so new anymore. Coming up on a year old already."

"How many kids does that make for you now?" Kellan's grin widened.

"Four. Two boys, two girls," Nathan said with satisfaction. "And Amanda's already talking about having a tiebreaker in a year or so."

Irina felt a sharp tug of envy for the home and family the sheriff had. She'd seen him and Amanda together at the diner she owned and they always looked…connected. Happy. She'd once dreamed of having that with Kellan, and knowing it wouldn't happen created an ache around her heart that throbbed with every beat.

"You know, Kel," Nathan said, getting serious again, "it's been good having you back in Royal. Usually you blow in and blow out again so fast, nobody gets a chance to say hello."

"Yeah." Kellan looked a little uncomfortable. "It was hard to be here before…"

"I get that," Nathan said, his features somber as both men remembered Shea and the legacy of pain she'd left behind. "But I'm glad to see you. Hope it's not the last time."

Kellan glanced at Irina, then back again. "I don't think it will be."

"Good to know."

Irina felt as if an entire conversation was going on between the lines of what she could see and hear. She didn't know what it meant, but she was willing to cling to hope just a little while longer.

"Anyway," Nathan said, getting back to business, "I'll make a few calls. Got a friend on Dallas PD. He'll go have a talk with Beckett and see if he can get through to him. If I have to, I'll go in and have a sit-down with him myself." He looked at Irina. "Don't you worry, though. He's done."

It was as if every tangled knot settled in her chest suddenly slipped free. Tension drained away and Irina finally released a breath she hadn't realized she'd been holding. When Kellan reached for her hand, she twined her fingers with his and squeezed briefly.

"Thanks, Nate." Kellan stood up and held out one hand to him.

Nathan shook it, then turned to Irina and shook her hand, as well. "I'll get on this today, so don't give your ex another thought."

"I won't," she said, though saying it and doing

it were two very different things. Until she heard that the police had taken care of him, Irina would probably still worry about Dawson and his threats.

"I'm sorry this happened to you, Irina." Nathan spoke solemnly. "It shouldn't have. Not in my town."

She shook her head. "It wasn't your fault, Sheriff."

"I've got a wife. I've got daughters," he said, his eyes holding hers. "Nothing pisses me off more, excuse my language, than some guy preying on women."

"Right there with you," Kellan muttered.

Irina smiled. Normally, she liked to handle her own problems. She hadn't been raised to wait for rescue, but rather to forge her own path—which, ironically, was what had gotten her involved with Dawson in the first place.

But she had to admit that it was reassuring to have the local sheriff ready to take care of her problems with Dawson. And if she were to be honest with herself, that was what it would take to get through to her ex. The man would never go away if it was only Irina demanding it. She never should have doubted that going to the sheriff was the right thing to do. "Thank you."

"You bet," Nathan said. "I'll call the Hollow to let you know when it's taken care of."

"Call her cell," Kellan said and gave Nathan the number. Then, catching her eye, he said, "Irina's going to Nashville with me for the weekend. I've got some business I have to take care of in person."

Well, this was a surprise. He wanted her to go away with him? Hope leaped up in her chest and Irina frantically fought to tamp it down. A weekend with him wasn't a future. It wasn't a declaration of love. And yet, she thought, it was more than Kellan had ever given before. "I am?"

"Aren't you?"

He looked at her and she saw that he wasn't issuing a command. He was asking. In the way that Kellan always would. She thought about it for a moment. Going away with him was only prolonging the inevitable. She'd give herself more to think about, more to miss. She'd add to the pain that would eventually find her when he left. She shouldn't dig an even deeper hole for herself, but how could she say no to a weekend away with the man she loved?

More important, why should she?

"Yes. I am."

"Perfect," Nathan said, completely oblivious to the undercurrents between Irina and Kellan. "This'll be straightened out before you two get home. And, Irina?"

She looked at him.

"I guarantee Beckett won't be bothering you again."

Lulu stepped into the foyer of Blackwood Hollow and shouted, "Miranda? Irina?"

"In here, Lulu."

Smiling, she walked into the great room and found Miranda curled up alone on one of the overstuffed couches. The twinkling white lights were blazing and the Christmas tree was lit against the gloom of the December day. It should have looked cozy. Welcoming.

Instead, Lulu took one look at Miranda and said, "Oh, honey, what's wrong?"

"Nothing, nothing." She shook her head and plastered a very unconvincing smile on her face. "I'm fine. What are you doing here?"

"Okay," Lulu said, dropping her black leather bag on the nearest chair before walking to join Miranda on the sofa. "Now I know there's something wrong. I'm here to pick up you and Irina for a fun-filled Christmas-shopping day at the Courtyard. The other girls and the camera crew are already there waiting for us."

"Oh God, I completely forgot." Miranda smoothed the wrinkled-up tissue in her hand and used a corner to dab at her eyes.

"It's no reason to cry," Lulu said, trying for a little humor. It failed miserably. "Sweetie, come on. Things can't be that bad. Just tell me what's wrong. Do you need me to go bitch slap someone?"

Miranda gave a short, choked laugh. "No, but thanks for the offer."

"Not a problem." Lulu paused and looked around the empty room. "Where's Irina?"

Waving that aside, Miranda said, "She's not here. She went with Kellan to Nashville for the weekend."

"Well, that's interesting." She tapped her finger

against her chin, then stopped and demanded, "Wait a minute. Did Kellan make you cry?"

"No," Miranda muttered in disgust. "Kellan made me furious and *that* made me cry."

"Man, I hate when I do that. It always makes me even more mad, which makes me cry harder. Vicious circle. So what happened?"

"What always happens when one of Buck's kids comes anywhere near me. Arguing. Name-calling. Tempers." Grimly, she shook her head and said, "I should just leave Texas altogether. That would show them all."

"Uh-huh." Lulu wanted to be supportive, but she needed more information. "Why?"

"I can't tell you, damn it."

"Why not?"

Miranda huffed out a breath and ground her teeth. "It's a secret. It's Buck's secret."

"Well, now I'm intrigued." Settling in, Lulu swung her hair back from her face, propped her elbow on the back of the sofa and stared at her friend. Miranda was always the composed one. The one of them who knew who she was and where she was going. She never failed to be coolheaded and rational. Seeing her like this was a little unsettling.

"How does a dead man have secrets?"

"If anyone could, it'd be Buck."

"Just tell me, Miranda. It's clearly upsetting you. So share."

Miranda watched her for a long minute, considering. Her eyes were still teary, but the expression on her face was pure frustration. "Can you keep a secret, Lulu? From everyone?"

Lulu didn't even try to laugh that question off. Miranda's gaze was straight and more serious than she'd ever seen it before. So she looked into her friend's eyes and said solemnly, "I'm a good friend, Miranda. I'm *your* friend. You can trust me."

She continued to study Lulu for another few seconds, as if deciding whether to continue or not. Then, decision made, she sighed. "I believe you. And maybe you're the one person I can confide in. Especially since you have no attachment to any of the people involved in this whole mess."

"You can tell me, Miranda."

Nodding she said, "Thanks for that. Okay, you already know that I got a letter from Buck, after he died, telling me to come here and about the will—"

"You mean about leaving you everything and ensuring his children will hate you? Yeah. I know."

"In the letter, he also said I could share this with someone as long as that person wasn't from Royal— which is why even Irina doesn't know what I'm about to tell you." Miranda gave her a weak smile, but at least the tears had dried up. "The thing is, I'm putting up with all of this crap and I'm not actually Buck's heiress."

Okay, whatever she might have expected, it wasn't this. "What do you mean?"

"I mean," Miranda snapped, "this is pure Buck. Even dead, he's pulling strings." She took a breath.

"He said I'd be receiving three letters. So far I've only got the first one."

"And what did it say?" Lulu was caught up in the secrecy of the whole thing. She'd had no idea people actually *did* things like this.

"He wants me to be the steward of his estate. Temporarily." She tore at the tissue, deliberately creating flimsy pieces of confetti that pooled in the lap of her black skirt. "I'm supposed to work with Kace—"

Kace, the yummy lawyer, Lulu thought and wondered when she'd see him again.

"It's going to take several months to straighten all of this out. Months where I get to be insulted, gossiped about and driven to total craziness." She shook her head fiercely, as if denying the whole mess. "But here's the really hush-hush part, Lulu. In the end—" she threw her hands up "—his kids are going to inherit after all."

"What?" This just kept getting stranger.

"Oh yes. Torture Miranda for months and then they all get their reward. Damn Buck anyway." Her eyes fired. "For example, Kellan's going to get this ranch, though he doesn't know it yet. And I can't tell him—so I have to put up with all of his bull, knowing that he's got no real reason to dish it out. Sophie and Vaughn will be inheriting a huge chunk of the estate, too, in spite of the way they're treating me, like I poisoned Buck to get all his money."

"This is so weird."

"Tell me about it. And before you ask," Miranda

added, "I'm doing this because Buck left fifty million to my charity, to compensate me for seeing this through. The damn man knew I'd put up with anything to see Girl to the Nth Power fully funded."

"Wow." Lulu laughed shortly. "I don't even know what to say to all this."

Miranda laughed, too. "That's a typical reaction to one of Buck's plans. You know, his kids hated me before and this isn't helping anything. This whole thing is driving me nuts. I loathe secrets and Buck knew that, damn it."

"Your ex really wins the prize, doesn't he?" Instinctively, Lulu took Miranda's hand and gave it a squeeze. "You're not alone in this anymore, Miranda. You've got me. And when things get tense, you can dump all over me, I promise."

Her friend laughed a little and gathered up the confetti from her skirt. She blew out a breath. "Thank you. Seriously, thanks. It really helps having you to talk to."

Lulu gave her a quick hug and said, "You know what else helps? Shopping. Why don't you go freshen up your makeup and we'll go meet the girls?"

"Right. Okay, I won't be long."

When she left the room, Lulu sat alone, her mind buzzing. She'd keep her friend's secrets, but she had to wonder if all superrich people were crazy, or if it had just been Buckley Blackwood.

Kellan wasn't sure why he'd wanted Irina with him on this short business trip. Hell, he didn't even know why he was planning on going back to Royal. Ordinarily, he'd have stayed in Nashville, gone back to his normal life. But now nothing seemed "normal" anymore.

It was a short flight to Nashville from the Dallas airport, just under two hours. But rather than fly commercial, Kellan preferred his private plane. Usually, he got work done during the flight, burying himself in reports, prospectuses and plans. But today was different.

Today, he had sipped champagne with the most beautiful woman he'd ever seen. If he felt a stab of guilt over that, because it seemed disloyal to Shea, he suppressed it. The two women couldn't have been more different, and it was as if he was only now realizing that.

Irina had a strength that Shea, in her more sheltered life, had never been forced to develop. Irina went her own way while Shea had done what was expected of her. At that notion he *did* feel disloyal, so Kellan shut those wayward thoughts down and focused on Irina.

"This place," she said, doing a slow turn on the teakwood porch floor, "is amazing. The house itself is beautiful and the grounds…" She shook her head a little and glanced over her shoulder at the yard, with its manicured lawn and surrounding trees. "It's like a painting. But…don't you get lonely here?"

"I'm not here often enough to get lonely," he admitted.

She choked out a laugh. "So you own a three-story house on five acres of land and you're not here often?"

He knew how that sounded, but he shrugged it off. "Most often, I simply stay in town at the Heritage Hotel. It's more convenient for work."

"Then why—" She waved both arms, encompassing the house.

"I guess you can take the boy off the ranch but you can't take the ranch out of the boy." It was a glib excuse, but one he'd used before. Kellan looked at the house, with its wraparound porches, elegant lines, and knew that buying it had been more of an investment than it was a true expression of him looking for a home.

He liked Nashville—hell, he owned half the buildings in the city—but it wasn't home and never would be.

Maybe he hadn't consciously admitted it before today, but the truth was, Texas was home. Royal, Texas. And more than that, his home was Blackwood Hollow. Funny that it had taken him this long to acknowledge that simple fact. Shea's death had chased him from Texas.

But now it was time to go back and fight for what was his. The question was, did that include Irina?

"Well, it's beautiful," she said and turned around to lean on the iron scrollwork railing. She lifted her face to the sunlight and sighed a little, simply enjoying the moment.

And Kellan enjoyed the view. She took his breath away. Punched at his heart and shook him right down to his bones. Irina wore a pale yellow dress with a full skirt that kicked around her knees paired with mile-high heels that did incredible things for her already gorgeous legs.

All he wanted to do was take her inside to the master bedroom and lose himself in the wonder of her for a few hours. But when she turned her head to him and grinned, he felt another hard jolt and knew that if he gave in to temptation, they'd never leave the bedroom all weekend. He had other plans.

When her cell phone rang, Kellan's thoughts shut off as Irina's features went tight and worried. Without glancing at the screen, she said, "That's probably Sheriff Battle."

Kellan hoped so, if only because hearing that Dawson Beckett had been dealt with would ease her anxiousness. He got up and went to her as she pulled the phone from her purse.

"It is him."

"Well, let's hear him out. Put him on speaker, Irina."

Nodding, she answered and said, "Sheriff, you're on speaker so Kellan can hear you, too."

"That's fine. Irina, I wanted to tell you that Beckett's been warned off."

She looked up at Kellan and he could already see worry draining from her eyes. "What happened?"

"That detective friend of mine in Dallas had a talk with Beckett. Told him in no uncertain terms to stay away from you."

"Will that work?"

Kellan dropped one arm around her shoulders and hugged her to him. If it didn't take care of the problem, Kellan would have a "talk" with the man and end this once and for all.

"It will," the sheriff said, "because Beckett's got a couple of legal problems at the moment already. He has a court date coming up in a week or two. So, if he bothers you again, he was told we'll add the attempted blackmail to his list of charges and that won't go over well with the judge."

She smiled and seemed to sag against Kellan. "That's wonderful. Thank you so much."

They could hear the smile in the sheriff's voice. "Like I said, it's my job and I'm happy to help."

"Thanks, Nate. We both appreciate it," Kellan said.

"Not a problem. Now, enjoy Nashville and I'll see you when you get home."

Home. There it was again, Kellan thought as Irina disconnected the call. Royal was home and it was resonating with him in a way it hadn't in years. Why now?

Even while he thought the question, he knew the answer was Irina. She had drawn him back into his family, into his hometown. What that meant, he wasn't sure—and didn't want to think about it now.

"I'm so relieved," she whispered, tucking her phone back into the tiny brown leather bag she wore draped on one shoulder. "I can't believe it. He's really not going to bother me again. Dawson, I mean."

"No," Kellan said, holding her shoulders and turning her to face him. "He won't."

"Thank you. For helping me with this."

He slid his hands up until he was cupping her face with his palms. He looked into her deep green eyes and something stirred inside him. "Dawson Beckett's out of your life, Irina. This time for good."

She took a deep breath and smiled. "I can't even grasp that. Not really. He's always been on the edges of my mind. Always a regret. A worry that somehow he'd find a way to reenter my life."

"Let it go now. Because you can," he whispered, and bent his head to kiss her. A slow, soft brush of the lips that had her sighing and swaying into him.

That unidentifiable *something* stirred within again and Kellan broke the kiss in response. He steadied himself and even then, the stars in her eyes when she looked up at him were nearly blinding.

They'd crossed a line in their relationship by coming to Nashville. Things were different here. *They* were different. Right here, right now, they were just two people with no past, no future. They had this weekend and it lay before them like a gift. Kellan was determined to appreciate every damn minute.

"I feel so good," Irina was saying and pulled away from him long enough to do a quick spin that lifted the hem of her skirt halfway up her thighs.

"Look good, too." He winked at her and she grinned, stealing his breath again.

"Thank you for bringing me here, Kellan." She

looked out over the grounds, then back to him. "You know, since I came to this country, I've never been outside Texas. This has made a lovely first trip."

"We're just getting started," he said and took her hand. "We've got a lot more to see."

"We do?"

Looking into those beautiful green eyes of hers, he could happily lose himself and everything else in the world that wasn't her. And Kellan wanted more than anything to keep that smile of anticipation on her face. There was so much he wanted to show her. Share with her. And no better time to start than now.

"One tour of Nashville," he said, tugging her along behind him, "coming up."

A few hours later, they were in a crowded bar, with flashing neon on the walls and country music streaming from speakers. Waiters and waitresses moved through the crowd like dancers, delivering drinks and laughing with their customers. And Irina took it all in with a big smile.

"You like country music?" Kellan asked. "I thought I knew everything about you and now you're throwing me a curveball."

There was still so much he didn't know, Irina thought. Like just how much she loved him. How much she wished they were any other ordinary couple out for the evening. But they weren't. There were secrets between them. And a ghost. And seven years of mistrust.

She'd been going along for the last couple of weeks, taking the days and nights for what they were. But she'd always known that things would change. This time with Kellan would end again, as it had so many years before. And when it was done, she wanted these memories. Wanted to be able to soothe her broken heart by drawing up images of him.

Deliberately then, Irina pushed all of those thoughts aside, because for tonight, she wanted the fantasy. She wanted to *believe*.

"I've lived in Texas since I came to this country from Russia," she reminded him with a smile. "So yes, I do like country music. In a lot of ways, the music itself reminds me of folk songs I grew up with, and that's comforting. I am a little surprised that you like it, though."

Both eyebrows winged up and mock insult was stamped on his features. "I'm born and raised in Texas, honey. Country music is sort of rooted into my blood."

Her smile softened until it became almost wistful. "That must be nice."

"What?"

"Growing up in one place. Feeling that connection." She sipped at her vodka again, then set the glass down. "My father died when Olga and I were very young and our mother moved us all over Russia while she looked for work. Being in Royal was my first try at developing…roots."

"Funny. I always thought that roots just tied you down."

"No, they anchor you," she said, wishing he could

see his home as she did. "You can go wherever you want, but there will always be a place where you belong. Where people know you and are happy to see you." She looked at him. "People in Royal have enjoyed having you back home. Your brother and sister especially."

He snorted. "Not Miranda."

She had to laugh at that, too. He and Miranda were truly oil and water, and it was a shame, because she thought if there weren't so many obstacles forcing them to see each other in the worst lights, the two of them might be able to be friends. "True. But Miranda is only there because your father wanted her to be."

"And we've circled around back to Buck," he said, sipping at his scotch as he leaned back against his chair.

She hated that every time his father came up in conversation, Kellan shut down. Yes, she knew that Buck hadn't been a perfect father. She knew that now, more than she ever had before. But at least he had cared. And Irina wondered if Kellan would ever accept that. Especially once he knew everything.

"He loved you," Irina said, feeling as though she still had to defend Kellan's father to him.

He smirked at that and had another taste of his scotch. "Had a strange way of showing it."

"His only regret was how he'd treated his children."

"Even if I accept that," Kellan said quietly, "it doesn't excuse him. Doesn't make me sad he's gone or wish for more time with him. Because frankly, every minute I ever spent with Buck turned into a contest of wills. The old man had a head like rock."

Her eyebrows lifted and Kellan grinned unexpectedly. What that smile did to her was lethal. How would she ever live without him in her life?

"Okay, so I inherited some of Buck's stubbornness."

"Some," she agreed, then tried to make him understand again. "Kellan, you have regrets. We all do. Can't you believe that Buck did, too?"

Before he could answer, the stereo shut off and live music erupted. They both turned to look down at the stage from their balcony table. A country band of five men in jeans, boots and hats were playing and singing and the crowd was already moving onto the dance floor.

Kellan stood up and held out one hand to her. "Dance with me."

He was full of surprises today and Irina was charmed. Everything about this trip had disarmed her. The private jet, his beautiful home, his easy smiles and the fun they'd both had touring this amazing city. But Kellan himself had touched her more than she ever would have believed possible.

He was attentive and sexy and funny and sexy and chivalric and sexy, and every second she spent with him made her love him more.

She slipped her hand into his, and when his fingers folded around hers, Irina felt the sharp blast of heat slam into her heart. As he led her down the stairs to the dance floor, all she could think was that when she lost him this time, the pain might actually kill her.

Ten

For the following week, Kellan fell into a pattern of filling his days with work and his nights with Irina. His assistant, Ellie Rae, kept him up-to-date with what was happening in Nashville via email, but for now, he was content to remain in Royal and oversee his businesses long-distance.

And the longer he stayed in his hometown, the less he wanted to leave it again. Even the ghost of Shea seemed less haunting. Maybe because things had changed enough that he was able to be in Royal now without expecting to see her around every corner. Or maybe, he told himself, it was simply time.

But everything in Royal wasn't rainbows and sunshine. There was still the will, Miranda and even the mystery of those four file folders he'd once seen in Buck's briefcase. He needed answers and Kellan wasn't going anywhere until he got them.

Sitting on a sofa in the great room, he briefly thought that by rights, he should have been behind the massive desk in Buck's study at the Hollow. Yet another reason to stay in Royal—fighting Miranda for his legacy. Grumbling under his breath, Kellan opened his email. He fired off some instructions to Ellie Rae, checked out a new property he was thinking of buying and then deleted a few emails from people wanting him to donate to whatever cause was the favorite that week.

He almost deleted the last email when he saw that it was from Dawson Beckett. He hadn't given the man another thought since Nathan Battle had called Irina in Nashville. So why was he contacting Kellan?

Against his better judgment, he clicked Open.

Blackwood, thanks to you and your bitch Irina, my businesses are folding.

Kellan smiled to himself. Good news after all.

Your daddy was a bastard and you're no better.

Chuckling now, he kept reading. If Beckett was miserable, Kellan was happy to hear all about it.

And speaking of bastards, Beckett continued,

got some news for you, boy. Your daddy left you
another brother.

What the hell?

Found out Buck's secret twenty years ago and held
on to it for the right time. Well, this is it, you son
of a bitch. Hope to hell it tears what's left of your
family apart.

Kellan slammed the lid of his laptop shut. Scraping one hand across his face, he stared at nothing
while his mind raced. Another brother? Was it true?
Buck had been a lousy husband and it was common
knowledge that he'd cheated on Kellan's mother regularly. But had there been a child?

And if so, why hadn't Buck done anything about
it? Was his soul really so small as to ignore his own
child?

Even as he considered it, Kellan knew it was very
likely to be true. Though Dawson wasn't exactly a
beacon of truth. Buck had ignored his legitimate
children. Why not one whom he could keep hidden?

But who, besides Dawson Beckett, knew about
this?

He stood up, stalked across the great room to the
wet bar in the corner and poured himself a scotch,
neat. He downed it in one gulp and relished the river
of fire filling him. His breath came fast and his brain
raced with information he had and speculation on
what he didn't.

Did Miranda know about this other sibling? Did Kace?

Did Irina?

In the week they'd been back from Nashville, they'd been together every night. Mostly she stayed at his ranch since there was no way in hell Kellan would stay at the Hollow as long as Miranda was holding court there. Irina had become an integral part of his life. Seven years ago, he'd run from the woman who he feared could make him forget Shea and the pain of loss. Today, he had been grateful for her.

Now all he could think was maybe it had all been a lie.

"Hell," he muttered, glancing at the bay window, "I even put up a damn tree because of her." The gigantic pine, regally decorated, shone with lights that he and Irina had strung themselves.

Briefly, he remembered that night and how they'd celebrated that tree, naked in his bed, with the door firmly locked.

And in all the time they'd spent together, Irina hadn't said a word to him about this. She'd never again spoken about those files that she'd brought him a couple of weeks ago. Never even hinted about the possibility of another Blackwood sibling.

But there had been *four* files in that case. Files she claimed that Buck had kept on each of his children. And that told Kellan she had to have known.

She'd simply chosen not to tell him.

He glanced at the time. Irina's night school class

had ended by now, so she'd be home soon. As anger rippled inside him, Kellan made a decision. Until he had more information, he'd be the one keeping secrets.

A few days later, the Texas Cattleman's Club was decorated for the season—and the annual holiday party.

Twinkling lights lined the branches of the trees in the parking lot and surrounding the club. Inside, the lights continued along the ceilings, and twined through pine boughs that lined the mantel and wound around the stair rails. There were several Christmas trees set up in different areas of the club with wrapped gifts destined for local charities gathered beneath them. Balls of mistletoe dangled from the ceiling on red ribbons and every white-cloth-covered table boasted red candles and a tiny vase filled with roses and pine sprigs.

Christmas music pumped through the speakers and everything seemed perfect—but wasn't. Irina was on edge. She felt as if her nerves had nerves. For the last couple of days, Kellan had been different. Quiet. Introspective. Cold. She'd caught him looking at her with speculation in his eyes, but when she asked him about it, he brushed her concerns aside. When they made love, he didn't hold her afterward, but rolled to his side and stared at the ceiling.

There was definitely something wrong, and the fact that she didn't know what it was was making her crazy.

She had thought that the two of them were be-coming closer. The trip to Nashville had done that, she thought. Because they'd had a chance to get away from everything that was hanging over their heads here, in Royal. Miranda, the will, Dawson. Secrets. Shea.

There was so much going on that at times it felt as if she were running in place. But since Nashville, she'd sensed a change in Kellan. He'd been happier, more open, more…involved than ever before. Until three days ago.

She missed that new Kellan. Missed that sense of rightness between them. She wanted him back. But she didn't know what to do to get him.

He was across the room from her at the bar get-ting them drinks. She picked him out of the crowd easily, though it had to be said that Royal, Texas, had more than its fair share of tall, well-built, gor-geous men.

Kellan wore a tuxedo as if born in it. His dark hair and beautiful blue eyes gave him a dangerous look that set off licks of heat inside her whenever she looked at him. Would it always be like that for her? She sincerely hoped so.

"Who are you checking out?"

Irina smiled when Lulu walked up. Though the party was a private one every year, meant for TCC members and their families, for some reason, the ladies of the reality TV show had been invited this year. Irina, for one, was glad of it. She enjoyed Lulu, Fee and Miranda.

Lulu's strapless, floor-length ice-blue dress skimmed her figure and outlined every curve. Her hair was done up in a twist at the top of her head while allowing soft tendrils to lie against her cheeks and neck.

"You look beautiful."

Lulu grinned. "Thank you. So do you. I love that dress."

So did Irina. It was dark red, with spaghetti straps and a deeply cut V bodice and a thigh slit. When Kellan first saw her in it, his eyes had flashed with the kind of heat that made her want to forget all about the TCC's annual formal party.

"So who are we watching?"

Irina smiled again. "Kellan."

"Ah… And, ooh, he's talking to Kace." She made almost a purring sound. "Isn't that interesting? Well, well, the lawyer looks very studly in a tux, doesn't he?"

"I suppose," Irina said and noted that Kellan was frowning as he talked to Buck's lawyer. What did that mean?

"Come on, Irina. I want you to see Miranda's dress. She went into Dallas to find it."

"All right, but—"

"Come on." Lulu threaded her arm through Irina's and pulled her along. "Kellan's not going anywhere. It's a party, remember?"

"You've got nothing to say about this?" Kellan demanded.

Instead of answering, Kace LeBlanc ran one finger around the inside of his shirt collar. "Why do they make us wear these damn things? Feels like I'm being hanged. Slowly."

"You're avoiding the question." Kellan had been gnawing on this other-sibling thing since that email from Beckett. He was unsettled. Uneasy. There was a cloud over him when he was with Irina now, because he couldn't be sure she wasn't working with Miranda against him.

He glanced over his shoulder to where he'd left Irina and saw her walking away with Lulu. Just that one look at her and his body tightened. His heart ached and he didn't like it. She was beautiful, though, no doubt.

When he first saw her in that red dress it had nearly knocked him out. Her long, silky hair was pulled back from her gorgeous face to fall in a curtain of curls down her back, and the thigh-high slit in her dress, not to mention the deeply cut bodice, was designed to drive him a little wild with desire.

Yeah. She was beautiful. And desirable. And so many other things that were now impossibly important to him. But was she treacherous, too? That was something he had to know.

Keeping his voice low, he demanded, "Damn it, Kace. Talk to me. Did my father have another kid?"

Kace looked around, to make sure no one was listening. He didn't have to, though. The banquet hall at the TCC was packed with what felt like the whole damn town. The noise level was just shy of deafening, so no one would be overhearing them.

"I can't talk to you about this, Kel," the other man said tightly. "I'm your father's lawyer…"

"Buck's dead."

Kace winced, then shrugged. "Yeah, I know. Doesn't end my responsibilities toward him and his estate."

"This is bull, Kace," Kellan insisted. "What about your responsibility to me? To Vaughn? And Sophie? We've got a right to know what the hell's going on."

Kace shook his head. "Not yet."

Frustration roared through him and Kellan had to fight to keep his temper in check. Last thing he needed was that damn camera crew swinging around to catch him in the middle of another argument. Besides, standing here giving Kace a hard time wouldn't do him any good anyway. He knew Kace. The man was loyal to a fault and as stubborn as Kellan himself. If he felt honor bound to stay silent, then there was no way Kace going to break a confidence—or the law.

"Fine." Admitting defeat, he nodded abruptly. "I'll find out on my own."

"Damn it, Kel," Kace said quickly. "Just leave it alone. Always so damn impatient."

"I think I've been plenty patient."

"God," Kace muttered, "it's like dealing with Buck again." Louder, he said, "You'll know everything eventually. Wait for it. You don't have a choice in this, Kel."

"Wait? You want me to wait?" he repeated. "How much longer? I've got Buck's ex living in the family home, inheriting *everything*, and now I'm supposed to quietly sit back and wait to find out if I've got another sibling out there? Really?"

Kace shook his head. "Yeah, I didn't really think you would."

"If you're not going to help," Kellan said, "then just stay out of my way."

"Well, don't do anything stupid."

Kellan just looked at him for a long minute. "*Stupid* would be to stand by and *trust* that everything will be fine. I don't do waiting."

He threw one last look toward Irina, surrounded by Miranda and the women of the *Ex-Wives* TV show, not to mention the camera crew. Miranda was here, so that meant he could get into the Hollow and look through Buck's office without being stopped or hassled. And if he was fast enough, Irina wouldn't even notice he was gone.

Standing in his father's office, Kellan half expected to hear Buck's voice telling him to get out. This study had been the old man's inner sanctum and no one was allowed inside when Buck wasn't there. Or when he *was* there. Or ever, really. Naturally, it had been the one room in the house that Kellan was always fascinated with.

"You can't stop me now," Kellan muttered as he walked to the closet. That was where Buck had kept his briefcase and so it would be the first place Kellan looked.

He found it, carried it to the desk and laid it

down. For a second he paused, because once he opened this case, there would be no going back. But to go forward, he had to know the truth.

The four manila folders were inside. Kellan set aside the ones labeled with his, Sophie's and Vaughn's names. Then he picked up the last one and opened it.

Darius Taylor-Pratt.

Kellan stared at the photo of a smiling man younger than himself, but with the clear stamp of their shared father on his features. Brown hair, brown eyes and clearly a Blackwood. He quickly scanned everything Buck had kept on the man and finally came back to the picture. There was no denying it. Darius Taylor-Pratt looked too much like Buck to even think about pretending otherwise.

Kellan had another brother. Another should-be heir to the fortune that Miranda had already stolen.

He thought about the lost years, time that he and his *three* siblings had lost. Time together they'd never have now. "Dad, you bastard. You should have told us. We should *know* our brother."

But then, there was a lot Buck should have done differently in his life. Gritting his teeth, Kellan used his phone to take a picture of Darius's file, then packed everything away again, set the case back in the closet and left the Hollow. Sitting in his car, Kellan tapped his fingers against the steering wheel as his brain ran with all of the new information. But there was one thing he kept coming back to.

Irina.

Did she know about Darius?

Was she in on all of this with Miranda?

Was her part in Miranda's plan to keep him so busy in bed he didn't ask questions?

Kellan needed to know.

Forty-five minutes after he left the party, he was back and scanning the room for Irina. When he spotted her, a flash of need jolted him. In spite of his questions. In spite of the sense of betrayal echoing inside him, everything in Kellan screamed at him to hold her. Kiss her. Touch her. Claim her.

Irina was on the dance floor with Kace, smiling and laughing up at his father's lawyer. Under the twinkling white lights, she looked ethereal. Like something that had stepped out of a dream. And yet all he could think was that she'd tricked him. Lied to him. Kept the truth from him.

And still he wanted her.

Pulse pounding, he stalked across the room, tapped Kace on the shoulder and said, "Cutting in."

His friend grinned. "I don't know, she's awful pretty."

Irina smiled up at Kellan and even as his heart turned over in his chest, he wondered how she could do that. How could she look so pleased to see him, if she'd been betraying him all along? Was she that good an actress?

"Yeah," Kellan ground out. "Find your own girl." He swept Irina into his arms, dismissing Kace without another thought. He steered her through the crowd, swaying to the music—some old song from the fifties, romantic, haunting.

The other dancers swirled past them in jewel tones, but he didn't see them. He could see only *her*. Irina's right hand in his, her left on his shoulder, she leaned into him and tipped her face up to his. She was so beautiful that, for a moment, he almost forgot the fury driving him.

All he could think was that he'd come so close to letting go of Shea. Letting himself love Irina. Had it had all been a game?

"Where have you been?" she asked.

"I went to the Hollow." He waited to watch her reaction, but all he read in her eyes was confusion.

"Why?"

"I had to get some answers," he said. "Now I have them—along with more questions."

"What are you talking about, Kellan?"

He dipped his head close to hers and whispered, "I'm talking about Darius Taylor-Pratt."

She stiffened in his arms and that told Kellan all he needed to know. He lifted his head and saw the truth written plainly in her eyes. She was aware of his half brother. Had known all along and hadn't told *him*.

"We need to talk," he muttered. Keeping a tight grip on her hand, he led her off the dance floor and through the crowded party room. He nodded to those they passed but didn't slow down.

If she said anything, it was lost in the rise and fall of the noise level in the building. Laughter, snatches of conversation came to him, but he ignored it all. He passed a couple under the mistletoe and wondered if there were secrets between them, too.

It was too cold outside for the conversation he wanted, so Kellan led her to the back, where the currently deserted childcare center was located. Drawing her into the room, he closed the door behind him and looked at her, trying to see her with new, more jaded eyes.

The room was filled with tiny chairs, short tables and colorful rugs. Shelves held what looked like hundreds of storybooks, and there were at least a dozen easels arrayed along the back wall, standing like soldiers waiting to be called into battle.

Irina rubbed her hands up and down her own arms as if she were chilled and he almost offered her his jacket, when he realized it wasn't cold she was feeling, but nerves.

"What's happening, Kellan?"

"Don't," he ordered, shaking his head and steeling himself against the shine in her forest green eyes. "Don't pretend you don't know. Not anymore."

For a moment, it looked as though she might try to put on an act after all, but then she sighed and admitted, "Yes, I knew about Darius."

"And didn't tell me," he ground out, feeling that hard slam of truth steal his breath.

"I couldn't," she argued. "It wasn't my secret to tell."

"That's crap, Irina," he said tightly, keeping a close rein on the temper pumping inside him. "You brought that briefcase—those files—to my house. You showed me my file."

"Yes," she said. "I wanted you to see it. To know that Buck cared. That he knew about you and your life. That you *mattered*."

Amazed that she was still defending what she'd done, he asked, "But you didn't think that my half brother mattered? Is that it?"

"Of course he does," she snapped. "You're putting words in my mouth."

"Because you're not telling me why you did this." He took a step closer to her and a part of him noticed that she didn't back up. Didn't retreat. And he admired her for it even while furious. "You should have told me, Irina. I had a right to know. So did Sophie and Vaughn."

"I know you do and you would have found out. When Buck wanted you to."

He threw both hands up. "Why do we care what the hell Buck wants? He's *dead*. What he wants doesn't matter anymore. The rest of us are still here. Still living. Still wanting answers."

Her chin tipped up and her eyes narrowed on him. "And you'd do anything to get those answers?"

"Damn straight." He pushed his jacket back and stuffed his hands into his pockets, more to keep from instinctively reaching for Irina than anything else.

Nodding, she locked her gaze on his and he read sorrow and anger there. "That's why you've been so good to me," she said quietly and Kellan was stunned.

"What?"

"This," she said, waving her hands to indicate her dress, his tux. "You asking me to this dance. You taking me to Nashville. Spending every night with me in your bed." She huffed out a breath. "God, I'm a fool again. It's all been a ploy, hasn't it? To get information about the will. To expose Buck's secrets."

"Are you kidding?" he demanded. "You're actually trying to say I'm the one who was sneaking around? Holding back information? *You're* the one who's been using *me*."

She laughed shortly and it sounded painful. "How? How, Kellan? Did I seduce you? Were you swept off your feet and made to feel important? Were you caught off guard by romance? Did you fall in love?" Her eyes filled, but she blinked the tears back, thank God.

Panic jolted him. "Who said anything about love?"

"I did. Weren't you listening?"

"Damn it, don't turn this around," he said. Kellan didn't want to think about *love*. Love wasn't the point. Trust was. "And don't change the subject. This is about you betraying me."

"No, it's not, Kellan," she said, slowly shaking her head. "This is about you finding a reason to leave. To walk away from me and whatever future we might have had in favor of clinging to memories of Shea."

"This isn't about her," he said, feeling a brand-new jolt of anger.

"It's always about Shea," Irina told him, walking closer so that she had to tip her head back to meet his gaze. She didn't back down from him or what she was saying. Instead, she stared him square in the eye and said, "You're constantly telling everyone 'Buck's dead,' expecting people to brush the man off and move on. According to you, he doesn't matter. His wishes don't matter.

"Well, Kellan, Shea's dead, too."

He flinched.

"You're not married to her any longer, Kellan. She doesn't decide your present or your future. She's your past. A big part of it and one that should never be forgotten. But you cling to her ghost. You use her as a weapon, to keep everyone else away from you." She drew a deep breath and said, "Congratulations. It worked. You're alone. You'll always be alone.

"And I feel sorry for you."

"I don't need your sympathy." How had this turned on him?

"You have it anyway. Because I love you, Kellan."

Pain shot through his chest, because it wasn't love he read on her features, but goodbye. And still she wasn't finished.

Her green eyes were shining with temper, sorrow, regret, and all three of those emotions reached for his heart and squeezed.

"You'll never know what it would be like to have

my love in your life every day. Neither of us will ever know what we might have had together. Because time after time, you choose the past over the future." She stepped around him and walked to the door. Opening it, she paused, looked back over her shoulder and said, "I wish you and Shea good luck."

Then she was gone.

Eleven

"He makes me so angry." Two days later, Irina was still fuming as she paced the length of Blackwood Hollow's great room.

"Yes, that's what men do," Miranda supplied, her gaze following Irina's every step.

"Well, Kellan is very good at it." She turned around to face the other woman, curled up on a couch in front of the roaring fire. "He thinks I lied to him."

"Well…"

"It wasn't a lie," Irina argued when she thought Miranda might see Kellan's side of things. Because she really hadn't lied to him at all. "I simply couldn't tell him the whole truth about Darius because it wasn't my secret to tell."

And yes, she'd felt guilty about that. Every time she was with Kellan and had to remain silent about his brother and other things she knew he would want to know, she'd felt pangs of regret. But she had owed Buck so much she couldn't break the promise she'd made him.

"I know that." Miranda held up both hands, one of which was holding a glass of straw-colored wine.

"Buck told me about his other son, before he died, Miranda. I think he needed to talk to someone. I blame Kellan for not understanding." And she did. It had been two days since the Christmas party and she hadn't heard from him. It was as if he had packed up his ghost of Shea and left town. But she knew he hadn't. Gossip was still the oil that kept Royal moving, so she'd heard that he was still on his ranch.

"Of course he's staying," she said to herself more than Miranda. "He won't leave until he gets to the bottom of everything."

The twinkling lights in the room seemed to mock her with their electric joy. Thanks to Kellan, she couldn't even appreciate the trees or the lights. Instead, they were all a reminder that she would be alone this Christmas, too.

"Just like his father," Miranda said wryly. "Ironic, don't you think, that Kellan considered his father a giant pain in the ass and he's turned out just like Buck?"

Irina dropped onto the sofa, picked up her own glass of wine and did what she could to wind down. It wasn't working, of course, because she could still hear Kellan's voice. Could still see the look in his eyes when he accused her of betraying him. He thought she'd been working against him. How could he believe that? How could he be with her and not know her—the core heart of her?

"I'm so angry and so—"

"Hurt?" Miranda offered.

"Yes," Irina admitted. "That, too. And disappointed. How could he believe I would do anything to deliberately damage him?"

"And we come back to… He's a man. They don't really think, you know." Miranda took a long sip. "For men, it's all about the penis."

Irina snorted her wine. "Excuse me?"

"Sorry, did I embarrass you?" Miranda didn't look sorry. "What thinking they actually do is done with their penises." She tipped her head to one side to consider. "Or is the plural *peni*? Doesn't matter. Anyway, it's all about whatever could be considered the 'manly' thing. What makes them bolder, stronger, richer. That's what drives them. It always comes down to size with a man."

"Miranda…"

"Sorry," she said again and this time it looked like she meant it. "I think I'm a little drunk. My point is, I am sorry you, too, are getting screwed by trying to help Buck."

"It's all right. I'll live."

Miranda groaned. "God, this is all such a mess."

"It really is." Irina agreed. "As far as my life

goes, this is all on Kellan. If he'd trusted me. If he'd waited. Given Buck the benefit of the doubt…"

"I get why he couldn't, you know." Miranda laid her head back on the sofa. "Buck could be a son of a bitch at times." She sighed. "When I first met him, I sort of liked that about him. He was the take-charge type. And I did love him, you know. Once." A sad smile crossed her face briefly. "But he didn't make it easy. And being one of his kids had to be more difficult than being his wife. At least, when I'd had enough, I could leave."

Irina knew that Kellan's father had been a hard man. But it wasn't all Buck was. And Kellan didn't have to carry on that tradition, did he? Miranda was right. Kellan was so much like the father he still resented and he just didn't see it. He could have come to her. Asked for answers instead of demanding them. Could have believed in her enough to listen. Instead, he chose to think the worst, and for that…

Her heart hurt. She felt as if she could hardly breathe. She hadn't slept since the party. All she'd been able to do was go over and over that last conversation with him. She wished it had gone differently. Wished especially that she hadn't told him she loved him, because now she didn't even have her pride to keep her warm.

Sighing, she took another sip of wine, looked at Miranda and said, "We're so wrapped up in the drama it's hard to see past it all. But, when this is all over, what will you do?"

"That's a very good question." Miranda studied her own wine and said thoughtfully, "I guess that depends on how it ends."

"He looks a lot like Dad, doesn't he?" Sophie studied Kellan's phone and the picture he'd taken of Darius Taylor-Pratt.

"'Course he does," Vaughn said, taking the phone from his sister. He glanced at Kellan. "We all do. Why should our brother be any different?"

"We have another brother," Sophie said with a laugh. "For me, another *older* brother. Yippee."

Kellan smiled briefly. Sophie had always complained about how he and Vaughn had hovered over her. Keeping the boys at bay, checking up on her all the time. He wasn't surprised at her attitude. "Yeah, you're still the baby."

"Great," she said. "Hey, maybe Dad has another one who's younger than me out there somewhere. I could finally get the chance to push someone around."

"Like you don't do that to us?" Kellan shook his head.

Sophie just smiled.

"Wouldn't surprise me to hear there are more siblings out there." Vaughn said. "The old man wasn't exactly a saint."

"True." Kellan took his phone back to study his half brother's face. It said something, didn't it, that none of them were really shocked at the news.

Buck had left behind a legacy of secrets. What was one more?

"So, does he know?" Sophie asked and Kellan smiled again.

She'd always had a soft heart. Of course Sophie was worried about how Darius was taking this.

"I don't think so. Not yet, anyway. Hell, *we* weren't supposed to know yet." And it still bothered him. How much more was there that he and his brother and sister weren't being told? Correction: *brothers*.

"Where does he live?" Vaughn asked. "Darius, I mean."

"California. Pasadena, I think the file said."

"Well, of course he doesn't live around here," Sophie put in. "If he lived anywhere near Royal, we'd already have known about him. No one keeps a secret in this town."

Except Irina. Kellan frowned to himself, remembering their last conversation. She'd looked hurt. Insulted. He pushed one hand through his hair, trying to somehow wipe her image from his mind. It didn't work, though. She was with him. All the time. Her smile. Her frown. Her voice. Her laugh.

Irina had become a part of him and without her...

"I like your Christmas tree," Sophie told him. "I'm surprised to see one in your house, but I like it."

He should have taken it down after that confrontation with Irina. She was the reason that tree was in the room and now every time he looked at it, he was reminded that she wasn't at the house anymore.

Kellan shot Sophie a quelling look, but as usual, it had no power over his sister.

"You did it for Irina, didn't you?" She gave a dramatic sigh. "So romantic."

Vaughn snorted. "A Christmas tree is romantic?"

"No," Kellan interrupted before the two of them got going. "It's not." Not anymore, anyway.

"So where is Irina these days?" Vaughn looked at him. "Haven't seen her lately."

"She's busy," Kellan said shortly. He didn't want to discuss any of this with these two. Hell, Kellan didn't want to even think about it.

But that wasn't happening. He hadn't been able to think of anything *but* Irina since that night at the TCC. He could still see her eyes, swimming in tears she refused to shed. The defiant tilt to her chin when she faced him down. And he heard her, too, in his mind, his heart. Heard her tell him she loved him when she'd called him out about dismissing his father after death and enshrouding his wife after she died.

He hadn't argued. Hadn't been able to. Because it was all true. He had done exactly that and it pissed him off now to realize that for seven years, he'd been stalwartly holding on to Shea's memory like a damn flaming torch. He always said he didn't want people's sympathy, but wasn't that exactly what he was silently demanding when he couldn't let her go?

God, his head ached.

"Hey, you don't look so good," Vaughn commented. "You're not mad about a new brother, are you?"

"What? No. Hell, he might be an improvement on you."

"Thanks very much." Vaughn slumped in his chair and took a sip of his beer.

"What about you two?" Kellan asked. "How do you feel about Darius?"

"I'm kind of excited by it," Sophie admitted. "I mean, when you're an adult, you don't often get a new brother or sister. So I'm looking forward to meeting him."

"What about you?" Kellan asked.

Vaughn shrugged and gave him a sly smile. "Hey, I'm all for having a younger brother for a change. Maybe I can order him around like you do me."

"Takes practice," Kellan warned.

"Well, hell, no wonder you're so good at it."

"So did you and Irina have a fight?" Sophie asked out of the blue.

Kellan looked at her. Were all women psychic?

"Just apologize for being a boob and everything will be fine."

Insulted, he asked her, "How do you know it was my fault?"

Sophie laughed. "Please. Of course it was your fault, Kellan. You're *you*." Shaking her head, she said, "You're as bossy as Dad was and just as inflexible sometimes. So apologize. Fix it. I like her."

"I like her, too," Vaughn said. "And yeah, it was your fault."

"Thanks for the support." Disgusted with his family, Kellan hoped to hell that when they finally met, Darius Taylor-Pratt would take *his* side for a change.

Apologize. He could. He'd been considering it for days.

But what if he hadn't been wrong?

Kace LeBlanc faced Kellan the next morning over a cup of coffee in the diner. Kellan wasn't really in any frame of mind for talking to his old friend, but when Kace called, asking for a meeting, he felt like he couldn't say no. Now he was second-guessing that decision.

"Why are you still working in the diner? How long does painting an office take anyway?" Kellan finished his coffee and set the mug down.

Kace shook his head. "Billy Talbot and his son are doing the painting—"

"Well, that explains it." Billy was good at his job but he was a notorious perfectionist. Painting the office could take a month or more.

"Yeah. But he swears he's almost finished."

Kellan really didn't care. "What's this meeting about, Kace?"

"About you and your inability to wait for a damn thing," Kace muttered. "I was asked to explain a few things to you."

"Asked by whom?"

"Not saying."

Kellan lifted his coffee and held it between his hands. "So, when *some* people ask you to do something, you do it?"

Kace sneered at him. "You know, I'm glad I went to school with Vaughn, not you. You're too damn annoying."

Kellan laughed shortly. He'd scored a point and they both knew it. "What are you supposed to explain?"

"It's about Irina."

"Nope." Kellan started to slide out of the red vinyl booth, but Kace stopped him. Kellan contemplated climbing over the leg blocking his way. It wouldn't exactly look dignified, but he wasn't about to sit there and listen to someone else tell him about Irina.

"Damn it, Kellan, listen to me."

"Why the hell would I?"

"Because if you don't, you're a damn fool. I'm willing to admit that you are many things, but I never figured that foolish was one of them."

"Fine." Kellan eased back and signaled Amanda Battle for a coffee refill. If he was going to do this meeting, then he needed the caffeine.

"Hi, boys," she said as she poured fresh coffee into their cups. "Anything else I can get you?"

"Not for me," Kellan said. He didn't plan on being there long enough.

"Once I'm done with Mr. Personality," Kace said, "I'll have bacon and eggs."

Amanda laughed, patted Kace's shoulder. "You bet."

When she was gone, Kellan said, "All right, talk."

"Irritating. Just irritating." He took a breath and

said, "I was asked to explain that Irina knows nothing about your father's will."

A knot in Kellan's chest tightened. "I didn't think she helped write it. But she did know about—" he glanced around the diner, making sure no one was listening "—about my *brother* and said nothing."

"She couldn't." Kace muttered something under his breath, clearly fought for patience, then said, "Buck told her about Darius before he died and asked her to say nothing. She promised Buck she'd do as he asked. I happen to know that when you give your word on something, you don't break it, no matter what."

"And that's important why?"

Kace looked exasperated. "Because for some reason, you expected Irina to break *her* word. You seem to believe that keeping it is a betrayal of you."

He hadn't thought of it like that, and he didn't much care for it now. She'd tried to tell him the same thing that night, but he hadn't wanted to listen. He'd been too wrapped up in his own anger—at his father, at the will, at the damn universe for keeping his *brother* away from them.

"Look." Kace kept talking and Kellan listened. "I don't know how much you know about Buck and Irina…"

He frowned. "I know some. She told me."

"Good. Did you know that Buck offered to pay for her schooling, but she turned him down? And after he died, she found out he had paid it all off, so she has no debt."

"Yes. She told me that."

"And Buck's the one who arranged a work visa for her. Gave her a job. A home. Somewhere to feel safe from that bastard she'd married."

Kellan idly turned his heavy coffee cup in circles on the tabletop. His heart felt like a lead weight in his chest. All of the things Irina had been through and survived humbled him. Hell, it made him proud of the way she had thrived. And as much as he hated to admit it, her loyalty to Buck was understandable, given his father's role in her life. "Yeah. I know most of that."

"And still you can get pissed at her for not breaking her word to Buck?" Kace looked amazed. "He was the one man in her life who helped her and expected nothing in return. The one man who offered her safety. The man who gave her a shot at a future."

"Damn it, Kace." Kellan was feeling lower than dirt.

"And on his damn deathbed, this man told her a secret and asked her to not say anything about it. She gave that man her word." Kace gave him a hard look. "And you give her a hard time for that? Call her out? What the hell, Kellan? You used to be better than that."

Kellan gritted his teeth and swallowed hard. He didn't argue, because how the hell could he? He'd come to most of this on his own already. Hearing Kace say it all out loud only underscored it. And made him feel worse than ever.

"Irina's sense of loyalty is every bit as strong as yours," Kace said. "You shouldn't be punishing her for it."

And that pretty much said it all, Kellan told himself. He'd given her grief for doing exactly what he would have done in her place. For three days, he'd been kicking himself for turning on her. For three nights, he hadn't been able to sleep because he needed her and he'd pushed her away.

He should have known. Should have realized that betrayal wasn't in Irina's nature. She was too loving. Too open, kind, in spite of what she'd been through in her life. And instead of seeing that, appreciating that, Kellan had attacked her for being who she was.

"I made an ass of myself," he grumbled and, man, did that cost him.

"Damn." Kace shook his head. "Never thought I'd hear you admit something like that."

"Yeah," Kellan grumbled, scraping one hand across his face. "Me, either. Didn't enjoy it."

"Not surprising." Kace shrugged. "But I'm not the one you should be saying it to."

He looked at his old friend. "You're right. I need to find Irina. But just know this, Kace. Our fight against Buck's will isn't over. Whatever happens between me and Irina... You and I aren't done."

Sighing, Kace only said, "Of course we're not. Now go away so I can have some breakfast."

Kellan slid out of the booth and marched out of the diner, headed for his truck. He needed to talk to Irina. Needed to tell her that he had been wrong. That he missed her. Needed her. And damn it, he wasn't going to lose her.

Irina needed to get out of the house. She'd moped enough. Missed Kellan enough. Now she needed to be with people, try to recapture her joy in the Christmas season and avoid all thoughts of Kellan.

"Good luck with that," she murmured, digging into her purse for the keys to the ranch truck.

The icy wind slapped at her and Irina tugged her coat closer around her. It wouldn't help, though, because since that last night with Kellan, she'd been unable to get warm. It was as if the chill in his eyes had seeped right into her bones. He was the one man she wanted and the one man who didn't trust her.

Shaking her head, she pushed him out of her mind. She climbed into the truck, adjusted the mirror, then stopped dead and stared as Kellan's luxury truck came roaring up the main drive like a dragon swooping in on a castle.

Her heart gave a solid jolt, but her mind sent a firm warning to keep calm. Inviting hope now would only make her feel worse when it didn't work out. He was probably coming to yell at Miranda again.

But he jumped out of his truck and ran to hers. He yanked open the driver's-side door, looked into her eyes and Irina's foolish heart began to hope.

"Thank God I caught you," he said. "We have to talk, Irina. Or I have to talk, anyway, and I want you to listen—no." He stopped, scrubbed one hand across the back of his neck and said, "I'm *asking* you to hear me out."

His eyes fixed on her and she realized that he'd never *asked* her for anything before. His hair was ruffled by the wind. He wore a dark brown leather jacket, a red sweater, black jeans and boots, and he looked so amazing, he took her breath away.

While he waited for her decision, she knew there was nothing to decide. Of course she'd listen to him. And she'd hope this conversation went better than their last one.

"All right, but let's go inside. It's cold out here." She grabbed her purse from the bench seat.

Kellan took her hand to help her down, then released her immediately. Irina curled her fingers into her hand because she missed his touch.

"Is Miranda home—never mind," he said, holding up one hand. "I don't care if she's there or not."

She smiled and shook her head. "She's not here. She went shopping. I was about to join her and the others. I want to buy some Christmas presents for my sister and her family."

"I'm glad I caught you, then." He took her hand again and led the way into the main house, through the foyer and into the great room.

"What is it, Kellan?" she asked, slipping out of her coat and tossing it onto the nearest chair. "What's so important?"

"You," he said quickly. "Us. We're important, Irina."

There went that thread of hope again. She clung to it and waited. Her heartbeat jumped into a wild gallop and she took a deep breath, trying to steady herself. It wasn't easy. Because she'd missed him so much, that just being near Kellan now was electrifying.

He came to her, and looked down into her eyes. "The other night, I was angry."

She laughed a little and folded her arms across her chest in an unconscious defensive move. "I know. So was I."

"You had a right to be," he said solemnly.

"Really." It wasn't a question, though she was curious about what had changed his mind. Why he was here. What had made him see the truth.

"Yeah." He scrubbed his face with one hand. "I'm sorry for all of it. If I'd taken the time to think it all through I would have known that you'd never trick me. Betray me. Lie to me.

"It's not who you are, Irina. And I should have remembered that."

Hope continued to grow in spite of the fact that she tried to rein it in. "I didn't want to keep that secret from you, Kellan."

"I know that. I do." Kellan laid both hands on her shoulders. "And I know that your relationship with my father was different from mine. I'm glad he was so good to you, Irina. I'm glad you had someone you could count on."

A sheen of tears filled her eyes and she blinked

them back frantically. Releasing a breath, she nodded and said, "Thank you. That means a lot to me."

His hands on her shoulders sent spears of heat shooting through her body and she welcomed it after the soul-deep cold she'd lived with for days.

"The truth is," he continued, "I don't think I ever knew the real Buck and that is a shame. But through you, I'm getting a different picture of my own father."

"I'm glad." She met his eyes and saw so many emotions shining there, she couldn't identify them all. And Irina wondered if her eyes were reflecting the same thing.

"Yeah, me, too," he said. "But I didn't come here to talk about Buck. What you said the other night, about Shea?"

"Oh, Kellan…" She still felt bad that she'd thrown those words at him—though she still believed he'd needed to hear them.

"No. Don't apologize. You were right." He took her hands in his. "I've been holding on to the memory of Shea for all the wrong reasons. I thought I was protecting myself, but I wasn't. I was hiding. And, Irina, I'm done hiding."

"What are you saying, Kellan?"

Behind him, winter sunlight pierced the front windows and lay across the floor in a soft golden pattern. The lights on the Christmas tree flickered, and in the hearth, a gas fire burned against the winter cold.

But all Irina could see was Kellan's eyes.

"I'm saying I love you, Irina."

She swayed under the impact of those words.

"I'm not afraid to say it anymore," he went on in a rush. "In fact, I want to say it every day. To you. I never thought I'd be in love again, but I am. And it's real and rich and everything to me. You are everything to me."

"Oh, Kellan, I love you so much."

"Thank God," he said with a choked laugh. "I was worried that I'd blown it completely. I'm so sorry I didn't listen to you. So sorry I didn't trust you."

The pain she'd carried for days began to drain away and Irina smiled up at him as he went on.

"You gave your word to my father and I respect that you kept it in spite of me being an ass."

She laughed again and covered her mouth with one hand to muffle it.

"You changed everything for me, Irina. Hell, I've got a Christmas tree in my house. But it's not Christmas without you. Come home with me. Be with me. Marry me."

"Marry you?" She blinked. He loved her and that would have been enough for her. But marriage? Family? This was the greatest Christmas gift she'd ever known.

"Yes. Marry me. Make a family with me." He cupped her face in his palms. "Irina, losing Shea broke my heart. You healed it. You brought me back from a dark, lonely place that I never want to visit again. Don't leave me out here all alone. Without you, I've got nothing."

Tears spilled from her eyes, but she was smiling at him.

"I know this inheritance fight isn't over—" He kissed her. "But it can wait. What can't wait is living a life with you. Marry me, Irina. Love me."

It was all she'd ever dreamed of. Kellan was here, loving her, holding her, promising her a shared future that looked so bright, it almost hurt to imagine it. Hope soared and love sailed with it.

"I do love you, Kellan. I always have," she said softly.

"So that's a yes? You'll marry me?"

"Of course I will," she said, joy bubbling up inside her.

He pulled her in tightly to him, wrapped his arms around her and buried his face in the curve of her neck. "You're everything to me, Irina."

Her heart was so full now, her chest felt tight. "Oh, Kellan, I've loved you since the moment we met. Nothing will ever change that."

"Then you'll come home and spend Christmas with me?" He straightened up and looked down into her eyes. "This one and every other one for the rest of our lives?"

"Yes."

He grinned. "I'll even ban Vaughn from the house so he can't storm in on us if you want."

Irina laughed again and it felt wonderful, to be so light, so full of wonder and hope and anticipation. "No, you won't. I love your family. All we have to do is remember to lock the door."

"Trust me on that." He nodded and asked, "So,

fiancée, do you want to go buy those presents for your sister? Because we could do some ring shopping while we're at it."

"A ring?" She swallowed hard, but it didn't stop the tears from flowing again.

"Of course a ring," he said, pulling her up against him again. "Any one you want." He kissed the top of her head. "And you know, if you'd like to deliver those presents in person, we could fly to Russia. Surprise your sister."

She stared up at him, jolted. Visiting her sister had been a secret dream, but one so out of reach she rarely even let herself think about it. "Are you serious?"

"I am," he assured her. "Or we can bring her and her family here for a visit, if you'd rather."

"Kellan, you keep touching my heart so deeply."

"Irina," he said softly. "You are my present, my future, my *heart*. Whatever you want, it's yours."

She smiled and looked into those beautiful blue eyes, seeing love shining back at her, and Irina knew that she'd already received the gift of a lifetime. Love.

"You, Kellan," she whispered. "I want you."

"I'm all yours, honey. Now and always."

As his arms came around her, she felt everything in her world slide into place. When he kissed her, she felt their souls link, felt their lives entwine and knew that this once-in-a-lifetime love was everything she'd ever dreamed of.

* * * * *

WE HOPE YOU ENJOYED THIS BOOK!

HARLEQUIN® *Desire*

Experience sensual stories of juicy drama and intense chemistry cast in the world of the American elite.

Discover six new books every month, available wherever books are sold!

#2707 RICH, RUGGED RANCHER

Texas Cattleman's Club: Inheritance • by Joss Wood
No man is an island? Tell that to wealthy loner Clint Rockwell. But when reality TV star Fee Martinez sweeps into his life, passions flare. Will their desire for one another be enough to bridge the differences between them?

#2708 VEGAS VOWS, TEXAS NIGHTS

Boone Brothers of Texas • by Charlene Sands
It isn't every day that Texan rancher Luke Boone wakes up in Vegas suddenly married! But when the sizzling chemistry with his new wife survives the trip back to Texas, long-held secrets and family loyalties threaten their promise of forever...

#2709 FROM SEDUCTION TO SECRETS

Switched! • by Andrea Laurence
Goal-oriented Kat McIntyre didn't set out to spend the night with billionaire Sawyer Steele—it just happened! This isn't her only surprise. Sawyer isn't who she thought he was—and now there's a baby on the way... Will all their secrets ruin everything?

#2710 THE TWIN SWITCH

Gambling Men • by Barbara Dunlop
When Layla Gillen follows her runaway best friend to save her brother's wedding, she doesn't know a fling with Max Kendrick is in her future. But when *his* twin brother and *her* best friend derail the wedding for good, Layla must choose between her family and irresistible passion...

#2711 ENTANGLED WITH THE HEIRESS

Louisiana Legacies • by Dani Wade
Young widow Trinity Hyatt is hiding a life-altering secret to protect her late husband's legacy, and wealthy investigator Rhett Bannon is determined to find it. But his attraction to Trinity might destroy everything they're both fighting for... or reveal a deeper truth to save it all.

#2712 THE CASE FOR TEMPTATION

About That Night... • by Robyn Grady
After a night of passion, hard-driving lawyer Jacob Stone learns the woman he's falling for—Teagan Hunter—is the sister of the man he's suing! As their forbidden attraction grows, is Jacob the one to give Teagan what she's long been denied?

Get 4 FREE REWARDS!

We'll send you 2 FREE Books plus 2 FREE Mystery Gifts.

Harlequin® Desire books feature heroes who have it all: wealth, status, incredible good looks... everything but the right woman.

FREE
Value Over
$20

YES! Please send me 2 FREE Harlequin® Desire novels and my 2 FREE gifts (gifts are worth about $10 retail). After receiving them, if I don't wish to receive any more books, I can return the shipping statement marked "cancel." If I don't cancel, I will receive 6 brand-new novels every month and be billed just $4.55 per book in the U.S. or $5.24 per book in Canada. That's a savings of at least 13% off the cover price! It's quite a bargain! Shipping and handling is just 50¢ per book in the U.S. and $1.25 per book in Canada.* I understand that accepting the 2 free books and gifts places me under no obligation to buy anything. I can always return a shipment and cancel at any time. The free books and gifts are mine to keep no matter what I decide.

225/326 HDN GNND

Name (please print)

Address   Apt. #

City   State/Province   Zip/Postal Code

Mail to the **Reader Service:**
IN U.S.A.: P.O. Box 1341, Buffalo, NY 14240-8531
IN CANADA: P.O. Box 603, Fort Erie, Ontario L2A 5X3

Want to try 2 free books from another series? Call 1-800-873-8635 or visit www.ReaderService.com.

SPECIAL EXCERPT FROM

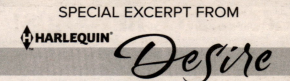

After a night of passion, hard-driving lawyer
Jacob Stone learns the woman he's falling for,
Teagan Hunter, is the sister of the man he's suing!
As their forbidden attraction grows, is Jacob the one to
give Teagan what she's long been denied?

Read on for a sneak peek at
The Case for Temptation
by Robyn Grady.

In the middle of topping up coffee cups, Jacob hesitated as a chill rippled over his scalp. He shook it off. Found a smile.

"Wynn? That's an unusual name. I'm putting a case together at the moment. The defendant, if it gets that far—" which it would "—his name is Wynn."

"Wow. How about that."

He nodded. Smiled again. "So what does your brother in New York do? We might know each other."

"How many Wynns have you met, again?"

He grinned and conceded. "Only one, and that's on paper."

"So you couldn't know my brother."

Ha. Right.

Still…

"What did you say he does for a living?"

Teagan gave him an odd look, like *drop this*. And he would, as soon as this was squared away, because the back of his neck was prickling now. It could be nothing, but he'd learned the hard way to always pay attention to that.

"Wynn works for my father's company," she said. "Or an arm of it. All the boys do."

The prickling grew.

"You're not estranged from your family, though."

Her eyebrows snapped together. "God, no. We've had our differences, between my brothers and father particularly. Too much alike. Although, as they get older, it's not as intense. And, yes. We are close. Protective." She pulled the lapels of her robe together, up around her throat. "What about you?"

Jacob was still thinking about Wynn and family companies with arms in Sydney, LA and New York. He tried to focus. "Sorry? What was that?"

"What about your family?"

"No siblings." As far as blood went, anyway.

"So it's just your parents and you?"

He rubbed the back of his neck. "It's complicated."

Her laugh was forced. "More complicated than mine?"

Shrugging, he got to his feet.

There were questions in her eyes. Doubts about where he'd come from, who he really was.

Jacob took her hands and stated the glaringly obvious. "I had a great time last night."

Her expression softened. "Me, too. Really nice."

His gaze roamed her face...the thousand different curves and dips of her body he'd adored and kissed long into the night. Then he considered their backgrounds again, and that yet-to-be-filed libel suit. He thought about his Wynn, and he thought about hers.

It didn't matter. At least, it didn't matter right now.

Leaning in, he circled the tip of her nose with his and murmured, "That robe needs to go."

Don't miss what happens next in...
The Case for Temptation
by Robyn Grady, part of her About That Night...series!

Available January 2020 wherever
Harlequin® Desire books and ebooks are sold.

Harlequin.com

HDEXP1219